A CHEROKEE PASSAGE

by

Karen Weinberg

WHITE MANE PUBLISHING COMPANY, INC.

This White Mane Publishing Company, Inc. publication
was printed by
Beidel Printing House, Inc.
63 West Burd Street
Shippensburg, PA 17257 USA

In respect for the scholarship contained herein, the acid-free paper used in this
book meets the guidelines for permanence and durability of the Committee on
Production Guidelines for Book Longevity of the Council on Library Resources.

For a complete list of available publications
please write
White Mane Publishing Company, Inc.
P.O. Box 152
Shippensburg, PA 17257 USA

Library of Congress Cataloging-in-Publication Data

Weinberg, Karen, 1950-
    Cherokee passage / by Karen Weinberg.
        p.   cm.
    Summary: In 1736 thirteen-year-old Ela draws strength from her
Cherokee heritage when she is kidnapped by Creek warriors.
    ISBN 0-942597-47-8 (alk. paper)
    1. Cherokee Indians--Juvenile fiction. [1. Cherokee Indians-
  -Fiction. 2. Indians of North America--Fiction.] I. Title.
PZ7.W43614Ch   1995
[Fic]--dc20
                                                         95-22699
                                                            CIP
                                                             AC

PRINTED IN THE UNITED STATES OF AMERICA

CONTENTS

CHAPTER ONE 1

CHAPTER TWO 11

CHAPTER THREE 25

CHAPTER FOUR 31

CHAPTER FIVE 36

CHAPTER SIX 49

CHAPTER SEVEN 65

CHAPTER EIGHT 87

CHAPTER NINE 99

CHAPTER TEN 115

CHAPTER ELEVEN 133

CHAPTER TWELVE 143

HISTORICAL EPILOGUE 148

FOR YOUR INFORMATION 151

ACKNOWLEDGEMENTS

I would like to thank the following people for helping me with this book:

Joan Green Orr, historian for the Museum of the Cherokee Indian in the Qualla Boundary, North Carolina (research expert).

Dr. Bill Anderson, Cherokee scholar and historian at Western Carolina University in Cullowhee, North Carolina (historical editor).

Charles and Randy Elder Booksellers, publishers of *James Mooney's Myths of the Cherokee and Sacred Formulas of the Cherokees.*

Diane Gordon (editor).

Lloyd and Evelyn Weinberg (my family editors).

CHAPTER ONE

On a chilly day in the early Spring of 1736, deep in the Smoky Mountains, a thirteen-year-old Cherokee Indian girl named Ela chased after her best friend.

"Please wait for me," Ela pleaded.

"Go away. Go back with the other children," Tewa insisted.

"But I want to come with you and the other maidens to gather clay. Now that they have finally let you join their group, they should let me, too. You are only four moons older than me."

"Please go back, Ela. If they see me talking with you, they may think I still want to be a child like you. I've waited so long to be accepted as a maiden. Don't ruin it for me." Maidens were young women of the village who were not yet wives or mothers, yet no longer considered children.

Ela could understand Tewa's desire to be accepted as a maiden. Ela also was tired of being treated as a child. It was different for boys. When they were about ten years of age, they were taken from the work in the fields to begin their training as hunters, warriors, and stickball players for the Cherokee Nation.

There were no such privileges for girls at that age. Not only did they continue to work in the fields, but they were also given the responsibility of caring for all the younger children in the village and were expected to learn the crafts of women. Maidens did less baby-sitting and more handiwork. Collecting boyfriends was also a favorite pastime for maidens.

Ela's life had little excitement. The small children she worked with often frustrated her. What would it be like to have the young men in the tribe look at her with love in their eyes? Ela sighed. To join the maidens, she would have to wait until she was invited.

"If you go back, I'll ask the maidens if you can join us next time we work together," Tewa continued.

Ela twisted a strand of waist-long, black hair around her finger. She would not beg Tewa any longer. "All right. But when you come back from digging clay, tell me everything you talked about. I want to know who everyone's boyfriend is."

Tewa smiled, gave Ela a quick hug, and said, "I promise." Then Tewa returned to her new friends. Ela turned toward the village, but she did not return to her child-care chores. Instead, she hid behind a cluster of mountain laurels and waited for a few moments. Then she quietly started to follow Tewa and the maidens. She wanted to know what maidens talked about when they were together.

Ela was far enough behind so that the maidens couldn't see her; however, she was able to hear their chatter not far ahead. The young women walked single file down the narrow path that ran along one of the many winding creeks that fed into the Little Tennessee River. Nequassee, her village, was located at the junction of the Little Tennessee and the Cullasaja Rivers. The surrounding majestic mountains were called the Shaconage by her tribe, which means "the place of the blue smoke." Her ancestors had lived in those mountains for countless generations. Ela had never traveled past the protective arms of this mountain range and could not imagine ever wanting to do so.

"Here we are," called out a voice from ahead of Ela. She quickly stopped. The maidens had approached a hillside that had been partially washed away by the flowing creek water, exposing the rich white clay that was found only in this part of the Cherokee Nation. It was the task of the maidens that day to collect as much clay as they could carry back to the village. Later, they would be expected to make the clay pots used to store food.

The worst of the winter weather was over. It would soon be time to prepare the fields for planting. The food storage sheds were almost empty, so the village men and their wives had gone off to the western foothills of the mountains to hunt for buffalo. They also valued the pelts of the buffalo which they used in trading with white men for metal tools and rifles. Women did not usually accompany the men on hunting trips, but it was necessary to prepare buffalo hides quickly to keep them from spoiling. This was woman's work. Many years ago, the buffalo had been numerous in the mountains and flat lands of North Carolina and Tennessee, but in recent years hunters had found it necessary to travel great distances to find the scattered herds that seemed to be migrating toward the West.

The only people left in the village were children, old people, and the young maidens. Food still needed to be prepared, firewood to be collected, and pottery to be made. The sick were to be cared for by the maidens because the village medicine man, who knew all the healing chants and potions, had gone with the hunters to keep evil spirits away from the hunt.

Ela looked after her grandmother when she wasn't needed with the village children. Grandmother, the mother of Ela's mother, looked very old. She had deep wrinkles on her face, permanent reminders of sixty years of smiling cheeks and worried brows. But most of the time Grandmother smiled. Ela believed that Grandmother was a happy person because she had so many adventures in her life. Listening to Grandmother recite Cherokee legends and tell stories about her life thrilled all the children in the village. Though the white-haired old woman could not speak much above a whisper, she was still able to capture the attention of her young audience. Her twisted arthritic hands gestured through the air as she spoke, her eyes looking off into the distance as though she could see the scene she was describing.

All the villagers called Grandmother "Beloved Woman." Most Cherokee villages had a "Beloved Woman," an old woman who had shown much bravery in her lifetime. There were times in Cherokee history when women had accompanied men as members of war parties. Grandmother had been on several raids of enemy villages and had once saved a wounded Cherokee warrior who was about to be killed by a Creek Indian warrior. Grandmother had charged at the Creek, screaming a chilling war cry as she ran. That distracted the enemy just long enough for the wounded brave to knock him down. Grandmother then killed the Creek with her tomahawk.

The "Beloved Woman" in each village was given the honor of making decisions about what should be done with prisoners taken during battle. Most of the time Grandmother would choose to let the prisoner join the tribe as an adopted member, but this was not always the case. Sometimes the prisoner was a particularly hated enemy, possibly a man who had killed a warrior from the Nequassee village. In that case, Grandmother would allow the village women to kill the prisoner. Ela did not feel bad about those times. That was just the way things were done in her village.

Hearing the words of the maidens was difficult for Ela as the young women chopped away at the clay wall with their sharp digging stones. Ela tiptoed as quietly as she could from tree to tree until she was hiding behind one not more than a stone's throw away from the maidens. The conversation was just as she thought it would be.

"I saw Nunda kiss Tsulu before he left on the hunt," said one of the maidens. The others all giggled.

"Are you going to marry him?" another maiden asked Nunda.

"I haven't decided yet," she responded proudly. "He has given me several small gifts. See the bear-claw necklace he made for me?" The maidens quickly surrounded Nunda and took a look. Ela strained her eyes to see the token of love.

"You always seem to have someone in love with you, Nunda," one maiden remarked. "I've tried to act more like you so that some man will notice me, but no one has even tried to kiss me."

Nunda sighed and calmly said to the less attractive maiden, "I'm sure more men will be attracted to you once I am married."

Ela thought Nunda was too vain. It surprised Ela that the other maidens should pay so much attention to Nunda since that only seemed to make the beautiful maiden more conceited. Conceit was not acceptable among their people. How could Nunda get away with it?

Suddenly, Ela was grabbed from behind by powerful arms. A strong, rough hand covered her mouth to keep her from screaming. Fear stormed through her body, but instinctively she thrashed her arms about and kicked her legs at the assailant. Feeling a finger near her lips, Ela tried to bite it. She was only able to get a bit of skin between her teeth, but it was enough to make her attacker pull his hand back for a second. In that moment, Ela let out a piercing scream.

"It's Ela," shouted Tewa, as she pointed toward her friend. She started to run to help Ela, but was pulled back by one of the older girls.

"Run. Tewa! Save yourself!" screamed the maiden. "We must warn the village."

Just at that moment, Ela could see another attacker start to chase the fleeing maidens. Nunda tripped and fell. "Help me!" she screamed, but the warrior was quickly upon her. He grabbed Nunda and carried her back toward Ela and her captor.

"Let me go! Oh, please let me go," Nunda cried.

With an unfamiliar accent, the man who held Nunda ordered, "Quiet, or you not live to see village again." That silenced Nunda. She stopped struggling, realizing that if the warriors were planning to kill her, they would have done so by now.

Out of the corner of her eye, Ela saw a short, slender warrior leading three horses towards his friends. The warrior holding Ela called out an order to his companions that made the men look around cautiously. They seemed nervous about staying too long in the clearing.

If only he knew there was no one left in the village able to rescue us, he wouldn't be so worried, Ela thought. Her captor bound her hands behind her back and then hoisted her up onto his horse, forcing her to lie on her stomach near the horse's neck. The warrior leaped up behind Ela, holding her in place with one hand while grasping the reins with the other. He urged his horse forward. Ela was unable to see much more than the horse's dusty brown coat and the passing ground from her position. She assumed Nunda was experiencing the same treatment.

The warriors raced their horses down the path, away from the village. The path left the small stream and soon led to the Cullasaja River which ran southeast from the village. The pounding of the horse's gallop knocked the breath out of Ela. Her ribs were already bruised, but she knew it would do no good to scream or cry.

"Where . . . are . . . you . . . taking . . . us?" Ela gasped. Her captor would not answer her. She realized it would be useless to ask any more questions. Eventually, the horses slowed down to a fast walk. Even though this allowed Ela to breathe more easily, her ribs were terribly sore. The only way to ease the pain was to lie as limply as possible so that her body blended with the movement of the horse.

Ela tried to think of something besides pain. She tried to picture Grandmother sitting on her bench in front of their cabin with sunlight shining on her silvery hair. She would have her buffalo robe about her frail shoulders. Maybe she would be wearing the moccasins Ela had made for her last year, the first pair of moccasins Ela had ever completed. They were not well made, but Grandmother had praised her efforts.

Poor Grandmother. She would be sick with worry by now. If Grandmother were younger, Ela was sure she would have tried to rescue the girls. Who would take care of Grandmother now? Mother and Father would probably not be back for several more days.

Then Ela heard Nunda whimpering. No matter how Ela tried, she could not see her. The warrior guarding Nunda made shushing sounds with his mouth to urge Nunda to stop complaining. Ela could hear him speaking to her in broken Cherokee. His voice sounded like that of a very young man, barely out of boyhood.

"Please let me sit up," Nunda pleaded. "I won't try to escape. I'm so sore that I'm sure my ribs will break if I don't sit up soon." The young warrior did not speak. "Please," Nunda continued, "I will be no good to you and your friends if my ribs are broken."

The young man cleared his throat, then trotted his horse up to the horse Ela and her captor were on. He spoke to the man in a foreign language, but Ela could tell he was asking the bigger man a question. She decided that her guard must be the leader of the group. The leader grunted a response and the small man pulled his horse behind Ela's. The other Indian who had been with the group was far out in front of the others, scouting the trail ahead.

"Sit," the small man ordered Nunda. Ela could see he gently helped the maiden change her position. Nunda was already getting favored treatment.

"Thank you," said Nunda so softly and sweetly that Ela could barely hear her. "I didn't think a man of your size would have such strong arms," she added.

Ela was shocked. What could possibly cause Nunda to be so nice to the enemy? If it were me, Ela thought, I would have spit in his face. Ela was already hoping she might get some broken bones so that the men wouldn't want her. She refused to beg for mercy. She would bear her pain in silence. After a while, her guard unexpectedly lifted her with one of his huge arms and set Ela in a sitting position. She felt guilty at feeling such relief from her pain.

Evening was rapidly approaching. They had been traveling for several hours. The high mountain peaks were blocking the sunlight from the path, and the glow of dusk could barely penetrate the forest ceiling. Ela felt cold. She tried to pull her blanket closer about her body. It was the red woolen blanket that Father had purchased from a trader. Very few members of her village owned woolen blankets. Most still used buffalo skins to keep warm. Mother and Father had left this precious blanket at home while they went on the spring buffalo hunt. Ela had dared to use it today hoping to get the attention of the maidens. She wore the blanket draped from her right shoulder, across her chest, under her left arm, and back up again to her right shoulder where it was pinned in place.

Nunda was wearing a short cape made of turkey feathers sewn onto fabric woven of plant fibers. Nunda's father was the peace chief of their village and he often wore a long turkey feather cape for rituals. Nunda probably got the idea to make her own cape from feathers as a way to look more important like her father.

It was so dark Ela could no longer see the horse behind her. Apparently, the warriors couldn't see either because out of the darkness ahead, Ela heard the scout call out to the others. His voice was calm, so there was no danger ahead. The scout rode up to the leader and guided him to a small campsite already pre-pared. The sight of a burning campfire started a rumbling of hun-ger in Ela's stomach.

Ela was pulled off the horse by the leader. "You, slave girl, sit." The man held on to her wrist as he brought her over to a tree several feet away from the fire. He bound her to the tree. Nunda was led to the same tree by the small man. He said with a stern voice. "You sit, too, slave woman." But after he tied her up he took off his own blanket and put it around Nunda to keep her warm. Ela felt disgusted.

The warriors pulled strips of dried meat out of their hip pouches and proceeded to eat in front of the girls. They gave no signs that they would feed their prisoners.

Nunda leaned toward Ela and whispered, "The man I rode with told me that we are to be sold to a white farmer to work in his rice fields. I've heard stories about others who have been sold into slavery, but that was many years ago. Since the Yamassee War, there has been almost no Indian slave trade."

"Then why would they want us?" Ela asked.

"The men who captured us are Catawba. The man I rode with told me that a white plantation owner offered guns and ammuni-tion for new female slaves. The white man thinks that women are less likely to try to escape than men. Maybe he needs more wives for his male slaves."

Ela was frightened. She no longer wanted to be a woman. If she had been a little smaller, she would probably not have been kidnapped. A stray tear rolled down her cheek.

"Are you hungry?" Nunda asked.

"Of course I am," Ela snapped. Nunda handed Ela a few strips of dried meat. "Where did you get these?" Ela asked.

"From my guard. He tucked it into the belt of my skirt before we got off our horse. He left one of my hands loosely bound so that I could use it to eat with."

"Can you untie me?" Ela asked with hope.

"I'd better not try. They'll be watching us closely."

"Then wait until they go to sleep."

"No, I think I have a better plan."

"What is it?" Ela asked.

"You'll find out soon enough."

Nunda shared her meat with Ela, feeding her like a pet raccoon. Ela ate her meat and then tried to fall asleep as quickly as possible. She didn't want to think of the future. She hoped for comforting dreams.

CHAPTER TWO

Ela dreamed that she was walking through a swirling, dark gray mist, wondering which way to go. Should she walk forward or wait to be found? Far ahead of her, the glow of a tiny light caught Ela's attention.

"Ela," whispered a voice from the glow. Ela could not tell if it was the voice of a woman or a man. She answered.

"Here I am. Who are you? I can't see you." She walked slowly toward the light. As she did, a figure formed itself out of the light. Ela's heart started to beat rapidly. It was Grandmother.

"Come to me, Granddaughter," she beckoned with her arms held out to Ela.

Ela started to run toward the figure, but the faster she ran, the farther away her grandmother seemed to be. A fierce wind started to blow against Ela, forcing her to work harder to reach her loved one. Hopelessness was tearing at Ela's heart, trying to find a way in. "Please help me, Grandmother," Ela cried.

Grandmother raised both her hands and clapped them three times. Instantly the mist and wind disappeared and Ela was safely beside the old woman. They stood hugging in front of Ela's home.

A chill rushed down Ela's spine though she knew holding Grandmother should have made her feel warm.

Grandmother said, "Sit and rest yourself," as she sat down on her own worn, wooden bench. As Ela obeyed, she thought to look around for her father, but when she didn't see him, she realized that her father was probably out hunting, for he was rarely at home during the daytime. Mother was not about either. She was a good mother, Ela thought, but Ela had always felt a closer attachment to her grandmother. It was probably because Grandmother seemed to have more time for talking to the growing girl. Mother was usually too busy with her many chores.

Ela put her head down on Grandmother's lap. Crippled, arthritic fingers combed Ela's hair away from her face and behind her ears. It felt soothing. Suddenly, Ela saw her mother, but Ela did not change position or even speak for fear Grandmother would stop stroking her. Mother never looked in Ela's direction. Instead, she concentrated on the work of scraping away bits of meat and fat she found adhering to the buffalo skin she was preparing for tanning.

Ela soon accepted where she was and began to relax. She realized that she hadn't enjoyed a peaceful moment like this since she was a young girl. Then she remembered something that had always made such moments special. "Grandmother, would you please tell me a story?"

Grandmother continued to stroke Ela as she proceeded to tell a favorite old tale about a handsome young hunter named Ataga.

One morning Ataga went hunting with his father. The two suddenly came upon a large buck. From where he stood, the young hunter was able to look right in the buck's eyes. For the first time, Ataga felt his brotherhood with the woodland animals. But before he could stop his father, the elder man shot at the buck with his bow and arrow. Ataga called out a warning to the buck, but it was too late. The buck was struck in the right hind flank as he tried to escape.

The young hunter, with tears brimming in his eyes, turned to his father, who demanded an explanation as to why his son should have acted in such an unmanly way, but the young hunter did not respond. Instead, Ataga ran after the wounded buck to see if he could save the animal. The buck ran swiftly even though he was wounded. Ataga could not keep up with the animal, but was able to follow his trail of blood droplets that had sprinkled on the brown leaves of the forest floor.

Many hours passed and at last Ataga could run no more. He came to a clearing in the forest. There lay a large oval patch of dried mud. Trees surrounded the patch. Ataga sat at the edge of the mud hoping that by chance the buck would return. He tried to communicate to the wild beast with his thoughts. He wanted to tell the animal that he was sorry that his father had hurt him.

Hunger tore at the young man's stomach, but he was determined not to eat until he had apologized to the buck. The night darkness surrounded him, but he refused to sleep, though his eyelids were heavy.

Finally, morning crept into the woodland. His first vision startled Ataga. Before him stood the buck, drinking from a crystal clear blue lake where before there had only been a mud patch. The arrow that had wounded the buck had fallen to the ground beside the animal. The wound was healed.

Afraid of scaring the deer away, Ataga whispered to him. From the hunter's mouth came a strange language, one that he had never been taught. He tried to speak words of apology but Ataga could not be sure the strange words that left his lips were saying what he wanted them to say.

The buck turned calmly toward the youth. The magnificent animal was listening. His eyes met those of the young hunter again. A voice seeped into Ataga's brain. "We are brothers you and I. I forgive you and your father. However, I must tell you never to come into this part of the forest again. This is the Lake of Healing from which only the sick or wounded ani-

mals of the forest may drink. Here is our place of safety and peace."

Suddenly, the buck ran into the forest and the lake instantly disappeared. The young hunter looked at the patch of mud. He thanked the Great Spirit for letting him see the buck alive. Then Ataga stood and followed the dried blood trail back to his land.

Ela knew the story was over, but she did not speak. She thought about how she had found her place of peace and safety.

Suddenly, Ela's dream ended when icy cold water splashed onto her face. She gasped and tried to dry her face on her blanket.

"Wake up, slave girl," ordered the leader of her kidnappers. Ela had not been able to see him well the day before. He had either been behind her or it had been too dark to see him. The broad shouldered Indian brave was about the age of Ela's father. His hair was worn short on the sides, leaving only a long lock of hair above his forehead that hung forward like a horse's forelock. There was another lock at the crown of his head to which was tied the wing of a redbird, and a lock at the nape of his neck hanging straight down like a horse's tail. His deerskin boots covered his legs up to his thighs, and he wore a breechcloth — a length of deerskin draped from the back of his waist, between his legs, and up to the front of his waist where it was held in place with a leather belt. His bare chest was partially covered with shaggy beaver skins loosely sewn together and draped over one shoulder with the fur side against his body. He was indeed a Catawba Indian. His tribe was a long time enemy of the Cherokee. He laughed at Ela's startled expression as he untied the captives.

Nunda had not gotten as wet as Ela, and she quickly stood up and arranged her clothing so she would not look disheveled. When Nunda tried to help Ela stand, the Indian brave pushed Nunda toward the surrounding forest and ordered her to bring him some water from the stream that could be heard nearby. He threw two hollow gourds to her to fill with water.

The Catawba who had scouted ahead of the others the day before came to Ela. He looked much like the first Indian but had numerous scars over his face. Ela stood up without help.

"Pick up blankets and put on horses," he ordered Ela. "I see if you good worker."

"May I have something to eat first?" Ela dared to ask.

"You ask me, Ochio the Warrior, if I feed you? You find own food. If you lucky, we give you water when Slave Woman come back." Ela cringed. She wondered what it was going to feel like to starve to death. Hopefully, this man was just trying to scare her.

The peaks of the surrounding mountains were capped with white patches of snow, but down at the foot of the mountain where Ela stood, the ground was cold and soggy. Ela picked up the three blankets that lay on the ground and placed one on the back of each horse.

The youngest warrior was tending to the horses. He had goose bumps on his arms from the cold. Ochio called out an order to the young brave. He obeyed immediately by running to the scout. Ochio ripped a budding branch off a nearby willow and handed it to the small Indian. The words Ochio spoke made the small man look very worried. Then the young man ran in the direction Nunda had gone. Ela believed he was going to see what was taking Nunda so long. Was he going to beat her?

Ela was ordered to hold the three horses still while the two larger braves swept the campsite with branches to cover traces of their stay there. Soon, the young Catawba and Nunda emerged from the nearby mountain laurel. Tears were rolling down the young woman's face as she handed the gourds of water to her captors. The small man looked proudly towards his partners as they nodded their heads in approval.

The leader drank several gulps and passed the gourd to Ochio. Ela was excruciatingly thirsty. She had tried sucking some of the moisture out of her wet blanket, but only a sip from one of the gourds would be able to meet her need. The leader threw the second gourd into the air toward the young brave. Much water spilled out before the gourd was caught. The older men laughed, then turned to prepare their horses for departure. The young brave took a sip and then held the gourd out to Nunda, but she refused and pointed to Ela. Because his eyes had been feasting on Nunda since their abduction, he had not really noticed Ela. Obligingly, he offered Ela a drink. There were only a few sips left in the gourd, but she savored them as the cool water coated her tongue and throat. She could even feel the water's coolness deep down inside her stomach. Then the young man took both gourds and tied them to a strap hanging from his horse.

The leader climbed onto his gray horse and Ochio mounted his tall brown stallion. The young brave held his head high as he climbed on his stout pony whose back was no taller than Ela's waist. The young warrior looked comical next to his friends, but he didn't seem to care.

Ela and Nunda were forced to walk ahead of the horses. Neither was allowed to speak to the other. Even the braves were silent as the group traveled along, following the stream slowly southward. Travel was difficult. Whenever small streams had to be crossed, the girls waded through on foot as the men rode comfortably on horseback. Ela's moccasins were soaked. Each time she stepped into a stream, water would fill her moccasin. The icy water numbed Ela's feet, causing her to trip on the rocks and fall to her knees. The lower edges of her leather skirt had gotten wet, making the garment heavy and uncomfortable. Fortunately, the skirt offered some protection from the chilling breeze. The wind had actually helped to dry her blanket, and she found comfort in the blanket's warmth and knowing that Nunda was also suffering.

Ela felt foolish walking ahead of her captors. She did not know where she was supposed to be leading the group. Frequently, the leader called out, "No, Slave Girl." Then he would point in the direction that he wanted Ela to turn. Soon after midday, Ela suddenly came upon a pheasant. It flapped its wings noisily as it tried to escape. The leader of the Catawba howled and jumped off his horse, bringing his bow and arrow with him. Ochio called orders to the young brave and then joined his leader. The two older men disappeared into the forest.

The young brave motioned for Ela and Nunda to sit next to a giant poplar tree as he stood at attention nearby to make sure they wouldn't escape. He was just far enough away that Ela felt he wouldn't be able to hear the girls talk.

Ela whispered to Nunda, "We've got to make a plan to escape." Then she looked quickly to see if the guard would be angry at the whispering. She was surprised to see that he was smiling.

"No worry. No hurt you," he said in broken Cherokee. "You no try escape. I be good to you."

Nunda replied, "We'll be good. Thank you for being so kind to me earlier today. I think you are a very brave man." The young man stretched himself up to appear taller as he leaned against a tree and started whittling a stick with his knife.

"How can you say that?" Ela whispered to Nunda. "He just beat you this morning, didn't he?"

Nunda smiled again at her guard and told Ela, "He just pretended to hurt me. We wet my face with spring water and rubbed my eyes red so it would look like I had been crying. His name is Essabo. Isn't he nice?"

"Nice? Nunda, he kidnapped us. Don't you want to try to escape?"

"It's much too dangerous," Nunda replied. "I think the best I can do is to make one of the warriors fall in love with me so he will keep me from being sold to the white men."

"How can you think of loving one of those horrible men? They have kidnapped us and we may never see our families again. I don't know about you, but when I get the chance, I am going to try to get away from them."

Nunda quickly said, "Oh, please don't get Essabo in trouble. He may be the only one who can help me — I mean us. I think he is starting to like me already." She smiled again at her possible rescuer and he smiled back.

Ela felt frustrated. Nunda was not going to be helpful, but if Ela tried to escape alone, Nunda would probably be punished severely. Ela didn't want that to happen. The farther the group traveled from Nequassee, the less sure Ela felt that she could find her way back.

Ela looked again at Essabo. She considered Nunda's plan. Maybe it would be smart to try make the men like her, too, but how would she manage that? She couldn't hide her hatred of the men and didn't know how to act feminine in the ways that Nunda knew. She decided she would try a direct approach. "Essabo, you must let us go. We'll die if we become slaves to the white men."

"You slave now. You no dead."

Nunda cleared her throat to get Essabo's attention, and when she had it, she stroked back her beautiful, shiny, black tresses and spoke. "If you take us back to our village, I will ask my father if he will let you stay with me there. My father is the village chief."

Ela watched Nunda give the young man an adoring look. He raised his eyebrows in surprise as Nunda stood and walked over to him, swaying her hips in the way only she could do so well. Just then, the leader and Ochio returned with two pheasants.

The leader frowned at Essabo and Nunda and pushed Nunda away from the dreamy-eyed brave. Quickly Essabo tried to give some excuse for their behavior to try to calm his partners. Furiously, the leader gave him orders, and Essabo quickly started to gather firewood.

Ochio threw the pheasants over to the girls. Nunda and Ela cleaned the birds and cooked them over the small fire that Essabo eventually built. There was not much meat left over after the braves ate, but the girls received enough to ease the sharpness of their hunger.

The journey resumed and they traveled for two more days under the same conditions. Ela had seen the chance for escape more than once, but each time she mentioned escape to Nunda, the maiden would tell Ela to wait. She would remind Ela that she was older and knew better. Ela could not be patient much longer. She feared they would soon arrive at their plantation prison. If Nunda made no move to escape today, the third day since their capture, Ela decided she would escape alone. The weather had been kind to the travelers. The sky was clear. They traveled mostly in a river valley with tall mountains on either side so that the sun was only visible during midday. The rest of the time they traveled in the shadows of the mountains and trees.

Ugly, red-headed vultures soared overhead and a few landed on the trees nearby. Woodpeckers tapped against distant tree trunks in their search for insects. The mountain laurel were not in bloom yet, but the tip of each branch had a swelling yellow bud where, in the summertime, there would be a beautiful light pink blossom.

Ela would have enjoyed the scenery if she wasn't so scared and miserable. Her moccasins had long since fallen apart. Her feet were well calloused from years of going barefoot, but the under-brush she walked through cut her ankles. Hunger was constantly gnawing at her stomach. This was a new sensation. All of her life, Ela had been provided a healthy share of all the food the village garden and nearby forest could produce. As Ela walked, she could feel her insides shrinking.

As the five travelers approached a bend in the river, they heard the blast of a rifle ahead of them. Ela's heart raced. Maybe she would be rescued. Quickly, Ochio ordered the others off the narrow path, as he jumped off his horse. Ela quickly screamed for help to whoever had fired the shot; but, unfortunately, a second shot drowned out the sound of her cry. In a moment, Ochio knocked her to the ground and covered her mouth. She tried to bite his hand, but he was holding her too firmly. He dragged her through the bushes to where his companions were hiding.

The leader held the horses and tried to calm them with petting and stroking. More gunfire was heard. This time it sounded closer. Ela looked to see if Nunda could scream for help, but Nunda sat quietly next to Essabo, who kept his arms wrapped around the young woman's waist. She didn't try to resist at all. Instead, Ela saw her snuggle a little closer to her new lover. Nunda whispered into the brave's ear and he smiled.

Another gunshot was heard. Out of nowhere, a dead squirrel fell at Ela's feet. Suddenly, through the bushes, a lone Indian hunter could be seen walking slowly along, poking his rifle in and about the bushes looking for his supper. When he got to the bush behind which Ela and Ochio were hiding, one of the horses whinnied. The hunter looked toward the horses with a surprised expression. Before he could run, Ochio released Ela and jumped out at the bewildered man. He hit him on the back of the head with the handle of his tomahawk, knocking the hunter senseless. Ela jumped up and ran, but the Catawba leader had been watching. He left the horses and chased after her, easily catching her.

"Bad. No run," he growled to her, his hot sour breath shooting into her face. Ela cringed with fear and revulsion.

Ochio rushed over to where Ela lay. He glared angrily at her, then unexpectedly smiled. He announced in Cherokee. "You earn us two rifles each if you so lively after many days of walking." Then he repeated what he had said in his own language with the same expression in his face and voice. The leader didn't seem to think it was amusing.

Ochio grabbed Ela, tied her hands, and put her on his horse. "No more escape," he whispered in her ear as he mounted the horse also.

Nunda mounted Essabo's pony willingly. The love-struck brave sat behind her. He did not bind her hands. Instead, he held onto the reins with one arm on either side of her. She would not be able to get away easily that way, and he could give her a hug once in a while when he wasn't being watched by the others.

Ela was glad that there was finally a reason not to walk any more; however, keeping her balance on the horse was a problem with her hands tied behind her back. All at once, her horse skittered to his left when he saw a rattlesnake sunning itself on a huge boulder. Ela was thrown off the horse and landed on her side with a thud. Ochio jumped down and, reaching out with his tomahawk in one hand, chopped the snake in two. Quickly, he reached down with his other hand to grab Ela and set her back on the horse. He looked at her with disgust and said. "You can't even stay on horse! You stupid." Ela kept silent as the brave tied a rope around her waist so he could hold on to her better.

They rode this way for hours. The river ran in the opposite direction of the way they were riding. Ela imagined herself gliding in a canoe toward home and pictured how happy her family would be to see her. She wondered if her parents had returned home from the buffalo hunt.

The river slowly narrowed until by late afternoon, it was nothing more than a mountain stream. Travel became even more difficult as they headed up the mountain toward the source of the stream. Eventually, they reached the crest of the mountain. The leader held up his hand to stop the others. Essabo rode forward to him, and they spoke briefly.

"We stop here," Ochio said to Ela. "Umpechy decide I guard you slaves while he and Essabo hunt food."

Umpechy. An ugly name to fit a despicable man. Ela was determined to remember all three of the warriors' names so that when she returned to her village she could tell her father which Catawbas to kill.

The men dismounted. Ela and Nunda were tied again to a tree. Ochio gathered firewood within sight of his prisoners.

Nunda whispered to Ela, "I hope they find a bear. I am so hungry I could eat one by myself!"

"Me, too," Ela replied. She tried to change her position slightly so that she wasn't sitting on the hard tree root that was bruising her bottom. Then she leaned toward Nunda. "Do you think we will ever get home again?"

"I think there is a chance," said Nunda. "Essabo told me how much he liked me while we were riding together. I'm almost sure I can convince him to leave his friends. If not, I will need to try to get one of the other men to like me." To prove her point, she spoke out to Ochio, who was busy carrying an arm-load of sticks to his growing woodpile. "You must be very strong to carry all that wood. I'll bet you are even stronger than your leader."

"Quiet," he replied.

Nunda didn't give up easily. "Oh, I didn't mean to say anything mean about him. I'll bet all of you men can be nice when you want to be."

"Leave me alone. I see how you try to trap Essabo. Your tricks no work with me — no work with Essabo either. He know we will kill him if he help you." Angrily, Ochio kneeled on the ground to build a fire. As he did, he coughed several times and then spit into the woods.

Nunda tried one more time. "I see that there are many sassafras trees around here. Would you like me to make a tonic for you from their roots? My mother makes it for me whenever I have a cold. It will cure your cough."

Ochio looked around to make sure his companions were not nearby, then he walked over to Nunda and untied her, leaving Ela alone. He told Nunda, "Need water for tonic. You get. I come too. Make sure you don't run."

Ela was left by herself. She felt pretty sure that Nunda had succeeded in getting Ochio interested in her despite what he had said. How did she do it? Ela felt like giving up hope. She had only succeeded in getting the men angry at her. There would probably be no more opportunities to escape now that she was being kept tied up. If only she were as pretty as Nunda, she might have had a chance. She was sure that Nunda had no concern for anyone else's welfare but her own.

Ochio and Nunda did not return as quickly as Ela had hoped, but when they did, the Catawba brave was laughing as he entered the campsite. When he noticed Ela eyeing him, he put a stern look on his face again. Nunda just smiled sweetly.

"I'm going to have to tie you up again," he said to Nunda, but he was much more gentle in his movements than he had been earlier. "I want the others to see that I guarded you well."

"Anything you say," she responded. Then Nunda looked at Ela, but the younger girl quickly looked down. She was furious. Nunda would probably escape slavery and Ela would have to suffer alone. It wasn't fair. The other two warriors returned to camp with a deer. They butchered it and cooked the meat while the girls watched. When the men were done eating, Ela and Nunda were untied and allowed to eat. Essabo brought the girls water to drink with their meal. He had noticed the warm looks that Ochio was starting to give Nunda, and he realized he had competition.

The campfire created an orange glow in the darkness of the night. Shadows seemed to bob from side to side as the flame flickered. Ela was exhausted and she lay on the ground to sleep with her hands and feet bound. She forced herself to concentrate on the journey taken thus far, to remember landmarks so that she could return home the same way. The men had purposely taken a difficult route to avoid any Cherokee villages along the main trading route. She closed her eyes to try to picture the place where the stream they had been following earlier that morning entered the river. She remembered having to step over an ancient fallen oak tree covered with brown moss not far from that location. Then other landmarks came to mind. She decided to be even more alert in the future and to test herself every evening.

CHAPTER THREE

"Where are they?" Ochio demanded as he grabbed Ela's arm and jerked her up to a standing position. The petrified girl opened her eyes and saw the warrior's atrocious face close to her own. She could see his blackened teeth as he shouted over and over again, "Where are they?"

"Where are who?" she whimpered.

"You know," he sneered. "Essabo and Slave Woman. They run away together. Tell me where they go or I throw you in stream."

As Ela came to her senses, she realized what Ochio was talking about. It was early morning. A quick look around the campsite confirmed that Nunda and her young admirer were indeed gone. Ochio continued with fury, "Tell me, Slave Girl!"

"I don't know where they went," she responded, more angry than scared. "If I had known they were leaving, don't you think I would have gone with them?" Ochio swept Ela up into his arms, carried her to the stream, and heaved her into the air. Ela screamed as she flew and landed half in and half out of the water. The muddy bank had padded her landing, so she wasn't hurt, but instantly she felt the icy water seeping through her clothing. With her hands and feet still bound, she had to wriggle like a snake to work her way out of the stream and mud.

Umpechy shouted an order at Ochio, then Ochio told Ela, "We be back to get you." The two men rushed into the woods looking for traces of Nunda and Essabo, leaving Ela alone, wet, hungry, and cold.

Ela squirmed her way up the creek bank and rolled over and over to reach the campsite. The campfire had not been rekindled, so it provided no warmth. She eyed a blanket which was still spread out on the ground. She maneuvered herself on top of it, then, holding one upper corner of the blanket in her teeth, she rolled herself up into it. There she lay, crying and waiting for her captors to return. She cried because she was truly on her own now. There was no older Cherokee to guide her. Even a selfish maiden like Nunda had been a better companion than none. Ela's tears streamed over the mud that was caked to her cheeks.

Eventually, despair turned to contempt. How dare those Catawba warriors kidnap her. It was a generally accepted Indian practice in wartime that captives could be used as slaves, but the men had not fought any war battle to win her. They had been cowards, ambushing her while the Cherokee braves were away from the village. Ela decided she would have to be just as sneaky to outsmart the Catawba. She would have to be careful, because if she was too hasty she might get killed. Determination to see her family again pulsed through her body.

The wool of the blanket drew the moisture out of Ela's clothes and held her body heat in. Her shivering body slowly became calm. Suddenly, a raven landed within a few feet of Ela's face. Ela kept very still so that she wouldn't scare the bird away. The raven cocked her head first one way, then the other, peering at Ela with curiosity. Ela wondered if the bird thought a girl wrapped in a red blanket might really be a huge worm or snake. The bird hopped closer to Ela's shoulder and pecked at it lightly.

"No, no, raven. I'm not your breakfast," Ela whispered.

The raven squawked and flew to a high tree limb overhead. Ela lay quietly, until the raven became less timid. Then Ela started humming a simple little tune to the bird which kept its attention. As she hummed, Ela slowly wriggled out of the blanket to show the bird that she was really a human. The shiny, black eyes of the bird reminded Ela of Grandmother's eyes. Had this bird been sent by the Great Spirit to let her know that Grandmother was thinking about her? Maybe Grandmother's spirit was in the raven.

The raven flew over the nearby tree from which hung a leg of deer meat left over from the night before. The men had put it there to keep bears away. With melodic gargling sounds, the bird picked at the food, then raised her beak high to swallow each morsel. Ela had never heard a raven make a singing sound before. She had only heard the loud croaking of their calls to one another through the treetops. Ela decided to try an experiment. She maneuvered her body into a sitting position and raised her face towards the bird, opening her mouth and imitating the sound a baby raven might make.

The raven looked curiously at Ela, undecided whether to fly away or not. The young Cherokee held her body very still and gave a more pleading cry. Finally, the raven grabbed a bit of meat and flew down to Ela's shoulder. The bird felt heavy and it was difficult for Ela to keep her balance. There was the possibility that the raven might start pecking at Ela's face, but instead, the bird dropped the food into Ela's mouth.

"Thank you," Ela whispered. Assuming the raven was female, Ela continued, "Such a good mother you will be some day. I think I will call you Little Sister. I've always wanted a little sister." Then Ela opened her mouth again and begged again. Back and forth the bird flew, bringing food to Ela. Suddenly, Little Sister flew up into the air and squawked loudly as she circled above the campsite. Ela wondered what had scared the bird away. She soon understood. A rustling sound coming from the forest let her know that her captors were returning.

The two remaining Catawba stomped into the campsite with angry faces. Nunda and Essabo were not with them. The men talked loudly to each other as they made large gestures with their arms. Ela guessed that they were deciding what kind of torture they would give the sweethearts when they were found.

Finally Ochio came over to Ela. "She was mine. Now we get only one gun for you." He picked up a handful of dirt and threw it at Ela. Ela knew that a gun was worth about twenty deer skins or 120 bushels of corn. Her father had told her about his trading ventures. These Catawba were not about to steal and carry that much corn to gun traders. There would be no time to gather deer skins and prepare them for sale.

Ela was set back on the horse and tied as before. She was glad she had eaten the food Little Sister had given her because the men never offered her any food that morning, though they frequently munched on the cracked corn that they kept in pouches attached to their belts.

The horses carried their passengers along a path that ran along the majestic mountain ridge. Ela looked behind her to get a last view of her tribal land. A tear rolled down her cheek.

"Cro-ack . . . cro-ack." Ela looked up, and there circled a raven high above the travelers' heads. Ela hoped that it was her friend, Little Sister. She was almost sure it was. The bird followed as Ela and her captors entered South Carolina.

Ahead of the travelers lay an enormous stretch of flat-land, a sight Ela had never seen or imagined. She was reminded of the only other long journey she had ever taken. Mother, Father, and Ela had traveled to Great Tellico, the new capital of the Cherokee Nation. There was a gathering to celebrate the coronation of Moytoy, the emperor. Moytoy had been appointed by Sir Alexander Cuming, a wealthy Englishman, who said he was the son of King George. Earlier, Cuming had recruited several members of the Cherokee tribe to return with him to England and visit the king.

Most of the men were from Nequassee, Ela's village. While they were in England, a treaty of everlasting peace had been signed.

Ela had enjoyed the two-day journey by horse to Great Tellico. When she first saw the town, she was surprised because it was much bigger than her own village. The town had a strong stockade around it built of tall, pointed oak poles to protect the village from invaders. Once inside the gate, she had seen the huge Council Meeting House. It had seven sides to it, representing the seven clans of the Cherokee Nation. Ela was a member of the Bird Clan. The other clans were the Wolf, Deer, Twister, Blue, Red, and Wild Potato. Ela had not been allowed to enter the meeting house, but her father told her there were benches lining the wall on which spectators could sit. He said there was enough space so that almost 300 people could attend council meetings.

A spacious playing field was located in front of the meeting house. It was on this field that Ela had watched some of her cousins play Chunkge with their friends. In Chunkge, a round, flat stone is rolled out onto the field, and while it is rolling, players try to throw long poles to the point at which they think the stone is going to stop. She had not been invited to play because she was a girl.

Surrounding the field were the homes of the villagers. Ela had been impressed to see that a few of the houses were log cabins like those of white men. Ela and her family had stayed in one. There had been no windows, just one door leading into the dark, three-room house. A fire burned in the center room, its smoke escaping through a small opening in the roof. The dark rooms were brightened by colorful hemp rugs lying on the floor and hanging on the walls.

Ela's daydreaming was interrupted by raindrops splatting on her head. She looked up and saw that gray clouds had filled the sky. Little Sister had disappeared. The intensity of the rain quickly increased. Soon the path the horses followed had become muddy and slippery. The travelers rode along a narrow, treacherous path winding between the base of a granite wall to their left and a steep hill to their right that angled down toward the stream twenty feet below.

"May I please have a blanket, too?" Ela asked Ochio. Her blanket was currently serving as a saddle for the man.

He just grunted and wrapped his own blanket tighter around himself. Ela started sneezing, and she found herself needing to lean against Ochio to keep as warm as possible. The wind was blowing harder and the air temperature was dropping rapidly. Shivers ran through Ela's body and she began to feel sick. Ela was frightened. If she became ill, there would be no one to care for her. She could die and none of her loved ones would ever know what happened to her. They would never be able to seek revenge.

Suddenly, a rush of energy flashed through Ela's body as she faced the fact that she would either be a slave for the rest of her life or she would die soon from pneumonia. To Ela, death was less fearsome than slavery. "If I am going to die, I will not die alone!" she screamed out. Ela gave the horse a mighty kick in the flanks and leaned her weight in the direction of the muddy slope where a quick death awaited her and her enemy.

Ochio tried to stop the horse, but it was too late. The horse fell over the hillside towards the stream. Ela was thrown from the horse onto the rocks in the stream. Before she lost consciousness, Ela saw the horse roll over on top of Ochio.

CHAPTER FOUR

Hot air engulfed Ela, making her feel as though she was suffocating. Her eyes popped open as she gasped for fresh air, but soon her panic subsided as she realized that breathing was possible.

The small, round room in which she lay was lit only by a small fire in its center. She vaguely remembered this room. It was the hot-house behind her family's home. The family hot-house had always been used to help heal family members who were sick, or to sleep in on very cold nights when the cabin wasn't warm enough. Ela could see that a large stone had been placed in the fire. It must have been very hot, because steam rose from its surface where someone had recently poured water. Ela blinked her eyes a few times to clear her vision. It was then that she saw Grandmother. Or was it Grandmother? This woman had Grandmother's face, but something was different. This woman looked younger. She had no wrinkles in her face. Her tousled black hair was hanging loosely around her face. Ela could never remember her grandmother's hair any way other than combed back neatly away from her face and tied into a knot at the back of her neck. But it was Grandmother's gentle touch that lifted Ela's head with one hand and poured a sip of herbal tea between Ela's parched lips.

"There, there, now. You just rest and I will take care of you," Grandmother said with a voice stronger than the old woman had demonstrated in years. As always, it sounded confident.

"Am I dying?" Ela asked.

"No. I believe you will live."

Ela wondered if this was a dream or if it was real, but she decided not to ask because that might make the dream end.

"Here, drink some more of this. It will ease your fever." Grandmother lowered a cup of tea to Ela's lips again. Ela took another sip of the bitter liquid. She didn't want to drink any more, but to please Grandmother and keep the dream going, she did as she was told.

"That's a good girl," said Grandmother as she lowered Ela's head back down on the buffalo skin bedding. Then Grandmother took a cool, moist cloth and wiped the sick girl's forehead with it. Ela closed her eyes and let the coolness penetrate into her fiery head. She wanted to stay like this and let Grandmother care for her forever. The danger of slavery was hopefully past.

"Oh, Grandmother, I was so frightened when I was kidnapped. The Catawba warriors wanted to sell me to a white man. I couldn't let them. I had to do something."

"Yes, my darling. I understand. There was a time when our people had never seen a white man. When I was young, I heard an old shaman, our medicine man, tell a story about a beautiful Indian maiden who was taking a walk to gather berries. Suddenly, she was confronted by several huge two-headed monsters. Each had one shining head set high above another long, ugly face. One of the shining heads shouted angrily at the maiden. All at once, the beast split in two. The upper half came down to the ground and walked towards her. She stood bravely to meet her fate."

"Did the monster kill her?" Ela asked.

"No," Grandmother answered. "She finally realized that the monster approaching her was a man dressed in heavy metal clothes. He had dismounted from his horse. Those were the first horses and white men our people had ever seen."

"What did they do to her?" Ela asked.

"They ordered her to take them to Echota where they had heard there was an abundance of gold. White men love gold and will do anything they can do to get it."

"Was the maiden a Cherokee woman?" Ela asked.

"No one is quite sure. She met the white men many days' journey from our land, but she knew all the secret paths to our land. I think she may have been a Cherokee who had been stolen by one of our southern enemies. On the journey to our country, the white men also kidnapped the Lady of Cofitachequi, the leader of many Indian villages in South Carolina. The soldiers thought she would have the power to assure them protection from natives they met along the way to Echota. The Cherokee maiden and the lady cooperated with the white men at first. It took them many days to reach our mountains. Late one night, while the men were sleeping, the maiden helped the queen to escape. The queen gave her some of her pearls as a reward."

"Did the soldiers ever find them?"

"No," said Grandmother. "The men were so angry that they rode further into our country and captured several braves to use as guides to help them find gold."

"Did they ever find the gold?" Ela asked.

"Not enough to make them happy. They traveled west and were not seen again."

"But what about all the white traders we see coming to our village? Where are they from?" Ela asked.

"They come from across the great water. They have great canoes with huge wings that carry them to our land. One of their canoes can carry as many braves as four or more of our canoes."

Ela could hardly imagine any canoes bigger than the long flat-bottomed dugouts the men of her tribe built. Theirs could hold up to 18 men. She had always enjoyed watching the young men at work making their canoes. First, they burned down a large pine tree or found one that had recently fallen and had not started rotting yet. Then, they stripped the branches and bark off the trunk and squared off all the sides. Those men who were lucky enough to have sharp iron tools from the white men were able to dig out a long narrow crater in the log to create a place to sit. Those who were not so lucky burned out a crater by laying glowing embers on the area to be hollowed. As the wood became charred, it was scraped away using a shell or hatchet. The embers were moved from spot to spot until the log was completely hollowed out.

"Do you trust white men?" asked Ela.

"I'm not sure. I imagine there are some white men that cannot be trusted, but there are probably many that can be. I have seen, in every tribe, a mixture of good people and people who are not so good. The white men are probably much like us in that way."

"White people frighten me," Ela admitted.

"Why?"

"Because they seem to want everything they see. I don't know if we will be able to control them."

"There do seem to be many things that are out of our control. That means we must concentrate on things we can control. We have to leave the rest to the Great Spirit."

"Which things do we have control of?" asked Ela.

"I believe we can have some control over how we feel about things. We can decide to be brave or to be frightened. We can decide how we treat other people and what we say to others. We can choose to have pride in who we are. No one can take these things away from us," said Grandmother.

"I don't know if a girl like me can be so sure of herself," Ela sighed.

"Don't underestimate yourself. You are almost a young woman, and you have learned much from watching and working with others while you were young. As you take on more responsibilities, you will find ways to manage them, and this will give you more confidence in yourself."

"I hope you're right," said Ela.

"Go to sleep now. You need your rest so you can get better. Remember, I love you," said Grandmother. She bent down and kissed her granddaughter's feverish cheeks. As Ela released herself to the nothingness of a deep sleep, she felt a cool flow of fresh air drift over her body.

CHAPTER FIVE

"I think she's starting to wake up now," said a young woman's voice.

"I sure hope so. I'm tired of having to tiptoe around here so that she can sleep," came a young boy's voice.

Ela did not recognize the voices. She wasn't sure whether to open her eyes or not. Then she heard a baby's cry. She quickly looked to see where the baby was. A tiny, wailing infant wrapped in soft deerskin lay on a fur mat not far from Ela. A girl, only a little older than Ela, sat on a wooden bench beside a young boy of about seven or eight. The girl looked from Ela to the baby, and then back again to Ela. She seemed to wonder which one to attend to, but was in no hurry to make her decision. The baby continued to cry.

"Aren't you going to hold the baby?" asked Ela. Ela always found it disturbing to hear a baby cry.

"I guess so," the girl said calmly. She stood and walked over to the infant. She brought the baby near Ela, sat down, and started to nurse the baby.

"So," said Ela. "The baby is yours?"

"Of course. Did you think it belonged to my little brother?" she laughed as she pointed to the young boy.

"No," Ela responded. She felt totally confused. She wondered where she was and who these people were. She felt sure she wasn't sleeping anymore. No one could have as terrible a headache as she did and still be sleeping. "Who are you?" Ela asked.

"I'm Anna Sluder Brown and that is my brother, Johnny Sluder, over there." Ela glanced at the boy again. He was filthy. His nose was runny. He wore only a long-sleeved cotton shirt that reached to his knees and a pair of ankle-high moccasins. His black hair was tangled and held bits of leaves and dirt.

Anna wasn't quite as offensive in appearance as her brother, but evidently neither had taken a bath in weeks. Her hair hung loosely about her face. Anna's and Johnny's skin was much lighter than Ela's, but darker than a white man's skin. Anna wore a dirty, white cotton blouse that had buttons running down the front, and she wore a full-length, brown, woven skirt that was gathered at the waist. She had tied a strip of leather around her waist to hold the skirt in place.

"Now, you tell us who you are. We've been wondering for the longest time. We were worried you would die before we found out," said Anna.

"I'm glad I didn't disappoint you," Ela responded. "My name is Ela."

"Why are you so far away from our tribe?" Anna asked.

"Our tribe? Are you Cherokee too?"

"Of course. Don't you hear me speaking your language? I could tell you were Cherokee from the clothes you are wearing. Actually, I am only half Cherokee. My father is a white man." She turned to her brother, "See, I told you she was Cherokee."

"Well, even if you were right, you should have told her my real name." Johnny turned to Ela and told her, "I don't want you to call me Johnny. Call me Mighty Panther! If you call me that other name, I'll hit you." He scrunched his face to look as terrifying as possible.

Ela tried hard not to laugh at the silly little boy. "I'll try to remember to do that, Mighty Panther. I don't need any more bruises." As she was becoming more alert, Ela was feeling increasing pain throbbing through her ribs and legs. She wondered if any of her bones were broken. Then the baby started cooing with satisfaction after her feeding.

"What's your baby's name?" Ela asked Anna.

"This is Zephyr. That's a pretty good name, don't you think?"

"Sure," Ela responded, though she had never heard such an unusual name before. Even the names 'Anna' and 'Johnny' sounded strange. "What made you name her Zephyr?"

"Zephyr is the name that sailors call a westerly wind. It is usually a soft, gentle breeze. My father was a cabin boy on a ship when he was young. He loves to talk like a sailor even though he hasn't been on a ship in years, so I thought he would like it if I named my baby a seaworthy name. I thought of naming her 'Ship Ahoy' or 'Shiver-Me-Timbers'." Anna slapped her knee and laughed at her own humor. "But she is so small and soft, it seemed that Zephyr would fit her better."

Ela wasn't sure what Anna was talking about, but she nodded her head. As Anna talked, Ela looked around the room and saw that she was in a decaying, wooden hut with gaps in the walls that allowed a brisk draft to push through. Dirty dishes and leftover food lay scattered about near the small fire.

"How did I get here?" Ela asked.

"I found you in the creek after the last big rain," said Johnny. "You seemed to be sleeping and I couldn't wake you up, so I got Anna to help me carry you here. You had a big bump on the side of your head. Once we got you dried off, your skin was as hot as fire."

Anna added, "You've been mighty sick for the past three days. Sometimes you would seem to wake up a little, and you would call out for your grandmother. I gave you broth to drink each time, and then you would fall back to sleep." Ela realized that the woman she had seen in her dream must have been a combination of Grandmother and Anna, a confused hallucination caused by her fever.

"Where are the men who were with me?" Ela asked.

"We only found one man, but he was dead. He looked like most of his bones had been broken. We buried him as best we could. We didn't have a shovel to dig with, so we pulled his body into the woods and piled river stones over him. I didn't think he could have been your father. He wore his hair differently than the Cherokee men."

"You're right. He was a Catawba named Ochio, and he and his friend, Umpechy, were going to sell me into slavery. I wonder why Umpechy didn't stay around to bury Ochio. Well, I guess I'm pretty lucky that they weren't such good friends because Umpechy would have found out that I was still alive if he had stayed. Did you find the horse of the dead man?"

"No," Johnny said. "Gee, if you hadn't been knocked out, you wouldn't have looked dead."

"I guess you're right," said Ela. She put her hand up to her forehead. It was moist from beads of sweat, but she had no fever. She tried to sit up, but was too sore and weak, so she lay back down. She watched Anna set her baby on her little bed of fur. "You do not dress like other Cherokee, Anna. Why is that?" Ela asked.

"These are the only clothes we have," said Anna. "We don't live among our Cherokee relatives. Our father is a white fur trader. Our mother is a full-blooded Cherokee from the Wolf Clan. We lived near the headwater of the Cape Fear River before we were captured and brought here by the Tuscarora."

"Oh, my. The Tuscarora are almost as fierce a tribe as the Creek people. I didn't know there were any in this area. I thought they had all been forced to join their Iroquois cousins in the North," said Ela.

"We thought so, too, but as we unfortunately discovered, there are a few remaining Tuscarora. The small group that took Johnny and me were planning to wait until spring to join their Iroquois relatives in the North. They just needed Johnny and me to help carry their belongings, do odd jobs, and cook for them until they could leave after winter."

"What happened to your mother and father?"

"I don't know. I was living alone while my husband was off on a trading expedition with my father. Johnny had come to stay with me for a few months to keep me company. My cabin is about a mile from the nearest neighbor. When the Tuscarora came, they had two warriors stand guard over Johnny and me while they attacked the other farms and burned the houses in our valley. I think we were the only prisoners they took. Fortunately, my parents live in another valley."

"Why didn't they kill you?" asked Ela.

"Probably because my brother and I spoke to them in their own language. My father has taught us to speak all the languages he uses when he trades with the different tribes. We were useful to them since we could understand their orders."

"Where are the Tuscarora now? Did you escape?" asked Ela.

"No, we didn't have time to escape. We prepared food and kept the Tuscarora camp in order until Zephyr was born. For the first few days after Zephyr's birth, one of the Tuscarora women brought fresh food to me. But on the fourth day, I stepped into the creek to wash my hands. When the woman saw me do that, she rushed back to tell the men that I had contaminated the drinking water. I didn't know that it was against tribal rules for a woman who has just given birth to use the stream above a village."

"The same is true for our tribe. I have been told that a new mother can make the water evil if she touches it. She must be sent away from the tribe or be killed."

"I guess I was fortunate that they just abandoned me instead. Before they left, they sent Johnny to take care of me. They were angry with him for having such a stupid sister, so they didn't want him to live with them anymore, either. He has been a big help to me," said Anna which caused Johnny to blush and shout, "Mighty Panther . . . Mighty Panther."

"What are you going to do now?" Ela asked Anna. "Will you go home?"

Johnny interrupted, "As soon as the baby is big enough to travel, we can go."

"When will that be?" asked Ela.

"I'm not sure," said Anna. "I've never taken care of a baby before. I never paid attention to how my mother took care of Johnny since I spent most of my time helping my father with his work back then. When do you think the baby can travel, Ela?"

"I think it depends on when you feel strong enough to walk a long distance. The baby just needs to be kept warm, dry, and fed. You can manage that while you are traveling. How old is your baby?"

"She is fourteen days old. I feel healthy enough to travel right now."

"Then let's go now!" Johnny exclaimed.

"Do you want to go with us?" Anna asked Ela.

"Yes, as soon as I feel a little better. Could you wait a day or two?" Ela asked.

"Of course. It will take us a few days to get enough food together for traveling. Do you know how to get back to Cherokee country?"

"Yes. I watched for landmarks the whole way here. We just need to find each one to get back."

"How will we find enough food to take with us?" asked Johnny. "There isn't enough time to dry meat. All we have here is that basket of corn meal. There aren't any crops at this time of year."

"What have you been eating over the past few days?" asked Ela.

Johnny answered, "Anna made tea out of plants she found. I caught two fish from the stream with my bare hands. Do you know how hard it is to do that?" Ela nodded. "Can boys my age do that in your village?"

"Not nearly as well, Mighty Panther." Ela assured him.

Johnny looked proud of himself. "Corn meal mush is about the only other food we have had to eat since the village stopped helping us."

"Do you have a blowgun?" Ela asked Johnny.

"No. I don't even have a bow and arrows. The Tuscarora wouldn't let us have any weapons."

"Then, we will make weapons. We can hunt for food while we travel. That way we won't have to carry so much. If you bring me some cane from near the stream, I could make a blowgun while I am still here in bed."

"Can you really do that?" Johnny asked excitedly.

"Yes," Ela responded. "I've been making them since I was your age. If you watch carefully, you could learn how to make a blowgun, too." Johnny started hopping up and down with joy as Ela asked Anna, "Do you have a long piece of fabric that you could use to bind Zephyr to you to help you carry her on the journey?"

"No. I'll just carry her in my arms. She doesn't weigh much. Of course, that will mean that I can't help you carry much of anything else."

"That's all right. Johnny and I won't need you to help us, will we, Mighty Panther?"

"No, I'm strong enough to do all the work myself. See my muscles?" Johnny flexed his skinny little arm.

"Well, I'm not quite strong enough to travel yet, so I'd better get plenty of sleep so I can get started on making our weapons tomorrow. By the way, is it morning or afternoon now?"

"It is late afternoon," said Anna. "Can I give you some corn meal to eat?"

"I'll try a little." Ela lay on her side and watched Anna scoop out a small bowlful of corn meal from their supply. Johnny brought Anna a bowl of water from the creek which she poured into a pot that was sitting near the cooking fire. Then Anna, protecting her hands with a piece of leather, picked up hot stones from the fire and placed them into the water one at a time until the water was boiling. Anna retrieved the rocks from the pot with a wooden spoon and poured the corn meal into the hot water to cook.

When the corn meal mush was ready, Ela took a few bites of the warm cereal. It was so delicious, she gobbled the rest down. Ela was happy to be feeling better and to have new friends.

The next day, Johnny brought Ela a choice of three straight poles from which she could make the blowgun. "Good work, Mighty Panther," Ela said. "Now watch what I do." First, Ela chose the straightest cane. The inside of the cane needed to be hollowed out. In the old days, Cherokee had used a pointed stone made of flint to bore a long hollow hole through the length of the cane. Sometimes, the cane was cut in half lengthwise, its inside was scraped out, and then the two halves were bound back together again. However, since the white man started trading iron to the Cherokee, most people used hot pieces of iron to burn the inside of the cane away. Ela had no iron with her.

"Anna, I need a small piece of iron. Do you have any here in the hut?"

"Not that I know of. All our cooking utensils are made of clay," Anna responded. "Johnny, where is your knife? Maybe Ela could use it."

Ela turned to Johnny. "You have a knife? Why didn't you tell me. That's wonderful!"

Johnny stood up taller with pride. "Daddy gave me this knife." He bent over and reached into his moccasin. He drew out a small knife case with a short child-sized knife enclosed. "My daddy told me to always keep this well hidden. That's why the Tuscarora didn't find it. You can use it, but you can't have it."

"Don't worry. I'll be very careful with it." Johnny handed the knife to Ela. She ran the blade lightly along her finger. It was very sharp. She carefully made a slit down two sides of a five-foot long, straight piece of river cane. The sharp edges of the severed cane made little cuts along Ela's fingers, but she kept working. She used a pointed stone to scrape the dried pulp from the inner core of the cane. Finally, she placed the two halves back together again and bound them with strips of dried animal intestines that she found in the food scrap pile outside.

It took most of the morning for Ela to make the blowgun. During that time Anna tended Zephyr. At midday, Ela took a nap while Johnny went down to the stream to try to catch a fish for dinner. Ela had asked him to also bring her some white oak splints by stripping long, narrow strands of wood from a recently fallen oak tree. With these, she could make darts for the blowgun. Johnny woke Ela up when he returned, his arms loaded with sticks, but no fish.

"Are these good enough?" he asked.

Ela looked at the wood very carefully. She set aside the wooden splints that would be too weak for darts and put the others in her lap.

"These are fine, Mighty Panther," Ela said. "We can make the darts today. I think we will make a fishing spear tomorrow and maybe a fish trap too. I know how difficult it is to catch them with your hands."

"I'll fix us some food while you two work," Anna said, but she mostly watched what Ela and Johnny were doing. Ela and Johnny made the darts by sharpening one end of each wood splint. To do that, Ela whittled the end into a point with Johnny's knife, and then she had Johnny rub the tip against a rough stone, slowly turning it as he rubbed to smooth out the edges. Normally, Ela would have tied fluffy thistledown from a bull-thistle plant to the other end of the dart, but this was not the season to find thistledown. She looked around the room for anything else that might work. She saw a worn blanket lying in the corner of the hut. It was different from the blankets she was used to seeing. This one had blocks of different-colored cotton fabric sewn into one large coverlet. The fabric looked puffy as though it was stuffed with something.

"What makes that blanket so puffy?" Ela asked Anna.

"You mean my quilt? It's stuffed with cotton batting. My mother and I made it. The Tuscarora let me wear it to keep warm when they took us from our home."

Ela noticed that bits of white fluff poked out of several tears in the fabric. "Could you hand me a few pieces of the batting so I can feel it and see if it will work with my blowgun? I need something to tie to the darts to keep the dart snug in the blowgun. Then when I blow on it, the air will build up behind the dart to push it out." Anna handed Ela a wad of cotton.

"This will be perfect," said Ela as she separated the strands of cotton with her fingers to make them more fuzzy like thistledown. She then took the dart and started to bind the cotton to the dull end starting from the top and working down several inches toward the middle of the wood using thread that Anna pulled from the seams of the quilt. Johnny watched Ela's every move and tried to do the same himself with another splint of wood. The first one he made was hopeless, but by the third try, he had a dart that might be usable.

By suppertime, Ela had completed ten darts. Johnny had made four. There was no longer enough light to see her work, so they stopped. Anna served corn meal mush and tea for supper. Ela's appetite was good and her strength was returning rapidly.

Johnny shoveled his food into his mouth as quickly as he could. He then announced, "Tomorrow, I'm going to go hunting with the blowgun and shoot a bear. I think I could eat the whole thing myself."

"If you see a bear, you'd better run," laughed Anna. "The bear may be hungrier than you are."

Johnny's eyes opened wide with fear, but then he realized Anna was joking. Looking angrily at his sister, he squatted next to the little cooking fire and poked a short stick into the embers to make them glow.

"I can hardly believe that we can go home," sighed Anna. "Everything is happening so quickly. It was a miracle that we found you to help us, Ela. We might have starved if we had tried to reach home by ourselves."

Ela had never had anybody depend on her skills before. It made her feel needed, but she was not going to act like she knew everything. After all, Johnny and Anna had saved her life. "I guess we needed each other," Ela responded. "I'm glad that there is a way to repay your kindness."

Zephyr started to cry, so Anna curled up on the animal skin near the cooking fire and nursed her baby to sleep. She had left the dirty supper dishes scattered about on the floor. Ela was too tired to be frustrated with Anna's sloppiness. Anna was already falling asleep with her baby.

"Johnny?" Ela whispered.

"Mighty Panther, you mean," he said.

"Mighty Panther, I'll bet you are glad you can go home soon. Don't you miss your parents?"

"Maybe a little bit, but I always wanted to live like my Cherokee relatives, and this is the first time I've had a chance to do it. My parents want me to act like a white boy. My mother says that white people are more civilized than Indians and that civilized life is the best way to live, but she's wrong. I don't like being civilized. I have to do chores all the time for my parents and wear uncomfortable clothes. I never get to do the things I want to do. I think that living like a full-blooded Indian would be the most exciting thing any boy could do. Nobody would make me do any work. I could spend all day hunting and fishing. I could learn how to be a warrior and learn how to walk through the forest without making a sound. I could learn secret Indian calls to signal other warriors."

"I don't think you know very much about Indian boys," said Ela. "When they are young like you, they still have to work in the village garden for most of the day. They have to help take care of the younger children, too."

"You're just saying that because you wish you could be a warrior like I'm going to be. I don't want you to talk to me anymore." The young boy pouted as he curled up on his fur mat. He gave a grunt as he dramatically turned his back to Ela.

Ela had never met such a stubborn child before. She wondered if he spoke as defiantly to his parents. His parents must be a little strange, too. How could they tell their son that being white was better than being an Indian? And what was that word, "civilized"? Ela decided to ask Grandmother about that word. The flickering light of the cooking fire reflected on the wall next to her with a hypnotizing motion. Ela closed her eyes and remembered to make herself review the landmarks for the journey home. Anna and Johnny were depending on her. Then she pictured herself marching victoriously into her village, leading Anna, Zephyr, and Johnny. Everyone would gather around Ela and beg her to tell them about her escape, but her grandmother would stop the crowd. She would say that Ela would need her rest after such a harrowing experience. The next day, the villagers would have a celebration, and Ela would tell them all about her adventure.

CHAPTER SIX

The morning air echoed with the chirping of the robins as they greeted one another among the trees. Johnny was still sleeping with his back turned toward Ela. Anna lay sprawled out on top of her mat several feet away from her baby.

Anna's behavior with her baby confused Ela tremendously. Never before had she seen a young woman so unprepared for motherhood as Anna. The young mother seemed to be a nice person, but she had no common sense about child care. Ela was used to admiring older girls and wishing she could be like them, but she did not envy Anna. She wondered if she could help her in some way. Maybe if she offered to help with Zephyr as much as possible, Anna could learn how to care for her baby by watching.

Ela stretched her body. She felt a surge of energy that assured her that she was no longer ill. It felt wonderful to be healthy again, and she looked forward to returning to her ritual morning bath. She had never been as dirty as she was now. If most white people bathed as infrequently as Anna and Johnny, it was not surprising that Indians could smell them across long distances. Ela could hardly stand her own odor.

She quietly stood up, found her blanket, and tiptoed out of the hut door, trying not to waken anyone. They needed their sleep to prepare for the long journey home. The outside air was very cold. The ground was coated with a layer of frost. There were a few spots in the clearings where the early morning sun was melting some of the frost. Next to the hut, the ground crunched under Ela's feet as she made her way to the stream. She pulled her blanket closer about her. Cold weather had never stopped her from bathing in the past and it wouldn't now.

At the stream Ela took off her blanket and skirt and laid them on a fallen tree trunk near the stream. Goose bumps immediately popped up on her skin. Ignoring this, she stepped into the water. The water was no colder than the air, but the iciness of it made her legs ache. The stones in the water were smooth and firm under her feet, but the water was moving so quickly, that Ela had to be very careful not to fall. The deepest part of the water was only knee deep, but that was deep enough to wash in. Ela scooped up handfuls of water and rubbed the water over her face and arms. The dirt on her body was not coming off well, so she picked up a handful of sand from the bottom of the stream and rubbed it over her body. The dirt peeled off layer by layer until she feared she might start to rub her skin off. She then dipped her hair into the water and ran her fingers through it. Particles of dried leaves and mud flowed out of her hair as the water passed through it. Ela shuddered to think she had been as dirty as Johnny. She stood up and flipped her hair back, slapping her back unintentionally with her waist-long hair.

Shivers ran through her body as she ended her bath and rushed up onto shore to wrap herself in her blanket. She rubbed the rough blanket fibers over her skin, which not only dried and warmed her, but also scrubbed off the remaining dirt. The sunlight had reached her fallen tree trunk, so Ela sat in the warmest spot, continuing to run her fingers through her hair to speed up the drying process.

As she sat there, Ela started planning her day. She and Johnny would have to make both the fishing spear and fish trap today.

Then Ela heard Zephyr cry. Ela quickly braided her hair and tied the end with a strip of fiber from the blanket. Zephyr continued crying. Ela wondered why Anna didn't quiet the baby. Maybe something was wrong with Anna and Johnny. Maybe the Tuscarora had returned and had done something to them.

Ela rushed back to the hut. Anna and Johnny were still sleeping. She could see the breathing movements of their chests, so she knew they were still alive. Zephyr continued to cry, but Anna just rolled over and pulled her blanket over her ears. Ela shook her head with disapproval.

Zephyr stopped crying as soon as Ela picked her up. The baby turned her head hungrily towards Ela. "No, no, little Zephyr, I'm not your momma, but I'll take care of you for a little while until your mamma wakes up." Ela took the infant out to the stream to give her a bath. When she took the blanket off the child, she couldn't believe how dirty the baby and the blanket were. In Ela's village, a baby would have moss padded around her bottom before wrapping a blanket around her. The moss would absorb any of the baby's wastes. The moss could be changed frequently to help keep the baby and the blankets clean. Apparently, Anna knew nothing about this.

Ela dipped the infant's little bottom into the water and Zephyr screamed in protest. Ela quickly washed the child, and then wrapped her up in Ela's clean blanket.

Anna came running toward Ela and the baby. "I heard Zephyr cry, but I couldn't find her. What are you doing to her?"

Ela opened up the blanket, revealing the now quiet baby. *So she really does care about her baby*, Ela thought. That was a good sign. Ela said to Anna, "I was just giving her a bath."

Anna cradled her child in her arms. She sat on the log next to Ela so she could feed Zephyr. "Why did you bathe her? Isn't the water too cold for a baby? I know it's too cold for me."

"My mother told me that everyone should have a cold bath each morning, especially babies. She said that the cold makes the baby's lungs stronger and keeps her from getting sick as she gets older. Didn't your mother teach you that?"

Anna shook her head. "I don't remember. My father certainly didn't take baths."

"Let me show you how to wrap moss in Zephyr's blanket so that she stays cleaner. I think she will stay happier for you that way."

"Anything to keep her from crying sounds good to me," said the young mother.

Ela found an outgrowth of moss growing on a rotting tree. She pulled up all of the spongy plant and laid it in a pile beside Anna. Then she took some of the moss and placed it around Zephyr's bottom before wrapping her in the blanket again. She washed the baby's soiled blanket and hung it on a nearby branch to dry.

"That looks like it will keep her clean. She probably won't need any more baths," said Anna.

"The moss doesn't work that well, Anna. You will need to change the moss several times a day to keep the baby clean and dry. And don't forget, Zephyr should be bathed every day. You might want to bathe with her. It would be more fun that way."

"We'll see," said Anna. "By the way, are you feeling better today? You look like you are."

"Yes, I think we will be able to complete our preparations today and leave tomorrow."

"What do you want me to do to help?" asked Anna.

"Can you make a fish trap?"

"No."

"Can you make fishing spears?"

"No," said Anna, looking worried. "I guess I'm not much help."

"Yes, you are. You could make our food today, take care of the baby, and pack our blankets and pots. That would be a big help."

"Good. I can do that!"

"Would you also collect any flint stones that you and Johnny may have? We will need them for starting our fires."

Before Anna started to get busy, Ela said, "First, let me hold Zephyr while you wash up. I'll meet you back at the hut." She turned toward the hut before Anna could object.

Hunger grabbed at Ela's stomach. She woke Johnny and together they made more corn meal mush. It was ready when Anna returned. Ela noticed right away that Anna no longer smelled bad, but she would need encouragement to wash her hair next time.

So that they would have plenty of corn meal to bring on the journey, the three limited themselves to one bowl of mush each. Anna started to put the dirty food bowls away into a tow sack. Ela stopped her and asked her to wash the bowls first. Fortunately, Anna did not complain. She seemed to like finding ways to be useful. Zephyr took a nap on her little mat.

"I'll go with you to the stream. I need to find some reeds that I can use to weave a fishing trap. I'll also need to find a river cane that is straight enough to make into a fishing spear."

Anna turned to her brother, "Johnny, you keep an eye on Zephyr."

"What will I do if she cries?" he asked.

"Just pat her back until I return. Ela and I will only be gone a few minutes."

"Oh, all right," Johnny said reluctantly.

Ela and Anna walked to the stream together. First, Ela cut a river cane from the area where Johnny had found the blowgun cane.

"Ela, I'm done washing the bowls already. Why don't you take the cane and the dishes back to the hut while I cut the reeds for your fishing trap. Do you think these will do?" Anna pointed to a heavy growth of reeds that looked pliable enough to work with.

"Yes, those are just right. Thank you. Here is Johnny's knife. I'll need about one big armful of the reeds."

"All right."

Ela returned to the hut. As she walked in the door, she saw Johnny trying to start a fresh fire for cooking. He held two flint stones and hit them together to make a spark, but he was having no luck.

"I'll do it, Johnny," Ela said, meaning to be helpful.

"No, I want to do it," Johnny insisted. "The baby seemed to be cold, and so was I, so I need to start the fire burning again. The only problem is that this stone here isn't sharp enough." He held one of the flint stones for Ela to see.

Ela set the dishes and river cane down and approached Johnny. "Here, let me help. That stone doesn't need to be sharp to work."

"Yes, it does," Johnny cried. Before Ela could reach him, he set the flint stone down on one of the rocks in the fireplace and tried to hit one edge of the flint stone with another rock from the fireplace.

"Stop!" screamed Ela. But the damage was quickly done. The flint stone had been crushed into dozens of unusable pieces.

"Uh oh," said Johnny, with his shoulders held up to his ears, trying to hide his shame from Ela.

"Johnny, I told you to stop! Now look what you've done. Can't you do anything right?" Ela was sorry as soon as the words left her lips. She knew Johnny had been trying to be helpful, but she was angry that a stone necessary to help them start fires had been ruined.

"I'm not Johnny! I'm Mighty Panther!" Johnny yelled.

"I'll call you Johnny if I want to," she said. Then she heard the baby start to cry. "See, you woke up the baby."

"No I didn't. You did when you yelled at me."

"Well, go hold her until Anna gets back."

Ela walked out of the hut and sat down in a sunny spot nearby. She hoped Anna had more flint stones somewhere. Their lives might depend on their ability to make a fire quickly.

Anna returned and set her load down in front of Ela. "Here are the reeds you wanted." Anna looked extremely proud of herself. She handed the knife back to Ela. "Where's Johnny?"

"He's taking care of the baby. She has been crying."

"I can't believe it's time to feed her again already," groaned Anna and she walked reluctantly back into the hut.

Now I can work in peace, thought Ela as she picked up the cane and started to carve a sharp point at one end. But in a few moments, Anna returned with Zephyr in one arm, and she held Johnny's hand with her free hand.

"Johnny told me what he did. He's scared that you won't let him help you anymore. I told him to apologize and see what happens." Johnny found it difficult to look at Ela, much less speak. She thought his chin might press right through his chest, his head hung so low. Anna urged him forward. "Come on, Mighty Panther. Apologize."

"I—I—I didn't mean to break the stone," was all the boy could say. Johnny looked so pitiful that he was easy to forgive. Ela remembered the times she had earnestly tried to help someone, and she had made mistakes.

"I know," said Ela. "I really do need your help, but you must listen to me and obey me when I tell you what to do."

The young boy lifted his head. "You mean you'll let me help you again?"

"Yes. Right now you can take the blowgun and practice shooting the darts towards a target. We may need you to do some hunting for us on our journey home."

"Really? I'm going to show you what a great hunter I am." He ran back to the hut and emerged with the blowgun and darts.

Ela showed him how to put the dart into the wider end of the blowgun. She held that end to her lips, with the cottony end of the dart close to her lips. She aimed the gun at a nearby tree. Then she took a big breath and blew quickly and forcefully into the tube. The dart flew out of the tube and hit the tree. It did not stick into the tree, but fell to the ground.

"If that had been an animal like a beaver or raccoon, it would have been stunned long enough for us to capture it. The dart could kill a very small animal, but your aim needs to be very good."

"Let me try. Let me try," Johnny begged. Ela handed him the blowgun. Then the young boy retrieved the dart and ran off into the nearby forest.

"Don't go too far," warned Anna.

"All right," came back the now distant voice.

"He's not such a bad little guy," Anna said to Ela. "Heaven knows he has tried to take good care of me."

"I believe you. I shouldn't have gotten angry at him."

"That's alright. He's pretty tough. My father has been hard on him. That's why I arranged for him to live with me at my cabin back home."

"What do you mean?" Ela asked.

"My father is not used to being around people very much because he travels for long periods of time alone. He has no idea what to do with small children. Whenever Johnny does something wrong or is hurt and starts crying, my father beats him. Sometimes my father has too much rum to drink, and then Johnny has to hide to avoid being hurt."

Ela could hardly believe her ears. In her tribe, children were loved. The fathers never beat their children. Among the Cherokee, a child belonged to his mother and her family. If discipline was needed, the mother's brother must speak to the naughty child. The worst punishment that could be inflicted was a little scratch on the child's arm with a porcupine quill. "Does your mother try to stop your father from hurting Johnny?" Ela asked.

"No. She's afraid my father will leave her if she says anything. She loves living in a sturdy log cabin and enjoys dressing in the beautiful fabrics that my father brings to her. He yells at her if she doesn't act like a white woman. He has convinced her that Indians are inferior people because they're not civilized."

"What is civilized?" Ela asked.

"That's a good question," said Anna. "Father seems to think that a civilized person is one who can read and write and knows about the rest of the world. He thinks people who are not civilized are no better than wild beasts."

"It sounds to me like he acts more like an angry beast than any person I know. Why do you suppose he married your mother?"

"I think it was convenient for him to marry a woman he wouldn't have to pay much attention to. Father really loved a woman named Molly in England. He and Molly were planning to get married, but before they could, his father died, leaving all the family debts to my father. Father couldn't pay, so he was thrown into prison for debtors. Molly came to visit him as often as she could, but she was poor and didn't have the money to free him. One year the English authorities decided the prisons were too crowded, so to reduce the prisoners in their jails, they decided to ship many of them to America. America needed more settlers anyway to work the land and send tobacco and furs to England. Father was shipped here to work as a servant for several years before he was free to start his own life. He never saw Molly again."

"That still doesn't explain why he married your mother."

"To Father, my mother is just a person who cares for his house and raises his children. Molly was his only love. Besides, having a Cherokee wife to watch over his house provides good protection from Cherokee war parties."

"No wonder he's angry all the time. Does he treat you as badly as he does Johnny?"

"He used to, but now I rarely see him. It was because of him that I got married. While we were out trading, he started grumbling to his new partner that raising two children was a big headache. Clyde offered to take me because his wife had died, and he needed a new one. At first father refused, but the next evening, they played poker. Father was losing and was about out of money. To keep the game going, Father said he would use me to bet with. Needless to say, he lost the game. At the end of the trip, I had to go home with Clyde."

"That's terrible. You should have refused to go."

"I didn't mind too much. It was almost worth it just to get away from Father. Clyde treats me well and fortunately isn't home very often."

"How old are you?"

"Fifteen."

"How old is Clyde?"

"Fifty-one," said Anna.

"Do you think that white people are better than Indians or half-breeds?" asked Ela.

"To tell you the truth, I don't think about it at all because I don't care. I just take care of myself, Zephyr, and Johnny. I don't care what color skin I have or anyone else has."

Ela heard Zephyr start to whimper. She realized she and Anna had been talking for a long time. There was still much work to be done. "I need to make the barbs on the point of this spear."

"I still need to find more moss for Zephyr."

"Why don't you set her on her mat out here in the sunshine," Ela suggested. "The air is becoming warmer. She will enjoy watching the sunlight play in the treetops. I can start making the barbs for the point of the spear and keep watch over Zephyr at the same time."

Anna got Zephyr and left her with Ela.

Ela was right. Zephyr cooed happily nearby as Ela carefully carved little barbs around the point of the spear. The barbs would hold fast to any fish that was speared. Anna soon returned with a small load of moss which she plopped down next to Ela, and then she watched Ela's skillful hands at work.

A rustling in the woods caught the girls' attention. Johnny called out, "Look what I did. Look what I did." When he came into view, he held a limp squirrel high over his head for the girls to see. "I told you I would be a good hunter." His smile was gigantic.

"Mighty Panther, how wonderful! You learn very quickly," said Ela.

"I'll cook the squirrel right now. We haven't had meat for much too long," Anna said as she took the squirrel.

"How are you going to build a fire? We only have one flint stone," Ela reminded Anna.

"No we don't. I have a few more here in my skirt pocket." Anna pulled out the stones to show Ela.

Ela was relieved. "Here," she said. "You'll need Johnny's knife to skin the squirrel." She handed Anna the precious tool. "We must guard this carefully. Without it, the food we catch on our journey will be too difficult to prepare, and we could go hungry."

"I'll be careful," Anna promised and she went into the hut. Soon smoke was coming out of the top of the hut as Anna cooked the squirrel. The squirrel was so small that each child only had a few bites of meat. Cornmeal mush had to fill the empty spaces in their stomachs.

After lunch Ela decided to take a short nap next to Zephyr. She wanted to be well rested for the next day's journey. She curled one of her arms around the sleeping child. What a soft, sweet baby. Some day she would have her own child, but not for many years. She wanted to explore the world first. The two slept peacefully for awhile.

Ela spent the rest of the afternoon making a fish trap. She took several of the reeds and laid them out on the ground to look like a star. Then she bound these into position with a thinner reed. In and out she wove other reeds, bending the outer points of the star up to form a basket shape. This basket was so loosely woven that Ela could see through the sides of it; however, the holes would be too small to allow fish to escape. That evening, the three children sat around their cooking fire. Zephyr lay cuddled in her mother's arms. Johnny was sleepy and he put his head on his sister's lap, but he fought to keep his eyes open.

"I'm not going to miss this place at all," Anna announced. "I can't wait to get back home. The first thing I am going to do is see if my parents are all right. Then I'm going to take Johnny and Zephyr back to my cabin. I'll have Johnny watch the baby while I sit on the porch and read a book. My father taught me a little ciphering with numbers to help him in his work, but a Quaker missionary came to our settlement last year and taught me how to read. He even gave me two books."

"What are books?" asked Ela.

Anna looked with surprise at Ela. "Haven't you ever seen a book before?"

"No," said Ela.

"Do you know what writing is? Do you know how to read?"

"I can read signs in the forest. I can read knife markings on trees to follow a trail, or animal footprints to find their dens."

"That's a little different from what I'm talking about," said Anna. "There is a way to make marks on paper to tell somebody something important or to tell them a story," she explained.

"I have seen picture stories painted on animal skins," Ela said.

"That's more like what I'm talking about. Instead of pictures, though, we can use letters to tell the story. There are twenty-six letters, or special markings, that stand for different sounds. When you want to write a word, you pick the letters that have the sounds that are in the word. Then you write them grouped to-gether to make the word on paper. Since stories have many words, writers often need several pieces of paper to tell the story. All the pieces of paper can then be bound together to make a book."

"What is paper?"

"Paper is like very thin pieces of leather."

"We use paint and sticks to paint our pictures. Sometimes we draw pictures into our clay pots with sticks while the clay is still soft."

"White people use feather quills dipped into a thin paint called ink. But I'm not good at making quill pens, and I don't have any ink, so I just use a stick that has been burned at one end. The charcoal makes a good enough writing tool for me. The only problem is that the writing smears if it gets rubbed. Lots of times I don't have any paper, so I write on the ground with a pointed stick instead."

The idea of writing thrilled Ela. She thought that if she could learn to write, she would write down all the stories Grandmother had ever told her. Then Ela could read them whenever she wanted to. And to think that Anna, of all people, actually knew how to do something special. "Can you show me how to write?" Ela asked.

"I can write words in English, but I can't write Cherokee words. There aren't any letters that fit the Cherokee sounds."

Ela felt disappointed. "Why aren't there any Cherokee letters?"

"I don't know. But if I teach you some of the English words, you can learn about writing and English at the same time."

Before Anna could have time to change her mind, Ela said, "Show me how to write the word for 'girl'."

Anna wrote the letters G-I-R-L into the dirt floor near the cooking fire. The glow of the flames provided just enough light for Ela to see the four letters. Then Anna pronounced the English word as she pointed to each sound the letters made.

"Show me more!" Ela begged.

"It's too dark to do this right now. I can teach you a few English words to say tonight while we fall asleep. Then I will teach you how to write them tomorrow when we have time."

"What words will you teach me?"

"Think about what you want to know as you get ready to sleep, then I will teach them to you."

The girls set out their sleeping mats. Anna lifted Johnny and placed him on his mat. He had fallen asleep as the girls talked. The hut was quiet. Frogs could be heard croaking along the muddy banks of the stream. A screech owl cried out to her mate.

"Are you still awake, Anna?" Ela asked after she had wrapped herself in her blanket.

"Barely."

"How do you say 'baby' in English?"

"BABY," Anna said.

"BABY," Ela repeated in English. She said it a few more times.

"How do you say 'boy'?"

Anna taught Ela how to say BOY and then went on to teach her the words MOTHER, FATHER, and GRANDMOTHER. Afterwards, Anna quizzed her for a few minutes to see if she remembered what she had been taught. Ela had little difficulty remembering the new words.

"That's enough for tonight," Anna announced.

"Can't we try a few more?"

Anna did not answer. Soon Ela could hear Anna's slow, deep breathing. The idea of learning English was very exciting. Now, Ela would be able to understand the traders that came to her village.

CHAPTER SEVEN

The day finally arrived for Ela and her new friends to start their long journey home. Ela felt like an eagle ready to take flight off a mountain peak. She longed for the sight of her family, the familiarity of her village, and the company of her friends.

Ela saw Zephyr wiggling in her blanket, so before the child had a chance to start crying, Ela picked her up and pulled her into bed next to her. Cold air blew through the hut and Ela could feel that the baby's skin was too cold. She held Zephyr closer, and soon the tiny body became warm. Zephyr seemed hungry, so Ela stuck her little finger into the baby's mouth. The infant sucked on the finger, making Ela giggle because it felt so strange. The baby's mouth was warm and soft. There were no teeth in Zephyr's mouth to scratch Ela's finger. Soon the baby went back to sleep.

Ela slipped out from under the covers to take her bath. As she walked to the stream, she remembered the English words Anna had taught her the night before. "BABY, GIRL, BOY, MOTHER, FATHER, GRANDMOTHER." Ela repeated these words over and over again as she splashed icy water over her body. She saw that the rhododendron leaves were curled tightly and angled closely to their stems. A person could tell how cold it was just by looking at the leaves. On warm days, the leaves stood out straight and flat. Ela decided it was too cold to wash her hair because it might freeze before it dried. She stepped out of the stream and rubbed her blanket vigorously over her skin to get dry and warm. Then she wrapped herself in the blanket and returned to the hut.

A loud crowing sound in a tree near the hut startled Ela. Looking up, she saw a raven. "Is that you, Little Sister?" she asked the bird. The raven tilted her head up to the sky, then looked back at Ela, seeming to shake her head "yes." Then the bird hopped down to the ground, far enough away to feel safe from the human, but close enough for Ela to know the bird was trying to get her attention.

"Little Sister, see? I have found friends who will help me get back to my people. Where have you been? Have you been busy building a nest?"

Little Sister hopped about the clearing and found a twig which she picked up in her large beak. Then she flew with it up to a tree branch.

"That's right, Little Sister. You can build your nest. The spirits have taught you how."

Little Sister shook her head and dropped the twig.

"Do you have a mate yet? That's all right if you don't. You will find him when the time is right. You are very beautiful." Little Sister squawked and flew into the dense forest.

"Who are you talking to?" asked Johnny as he came out of the hut.

"It's a raven who became my friend when the Catawba braves were being so cruel to me. I guess she followed me here. I named her Little Sister."

"I never heard of anyone having a pet raven. You sure are lucky," Johnny said. He strained his eyes to catch a glimpse of Little Sister, but she was out of sight. He said to Ela, "Let's leave soon. I want to go home . . . I mean I want to go to your village."

"Johnny, which place would you really like to go to? I know Anna wants you to go home with her."

"I want to be an Indian brave. I will go with you to the village." Johnny crossed his arms in front of his chest and looked defiantly at Ela.

"I'm not sure that's a good idea, but we can decide about that later. First, we must eat and then finish packing our supplies. Wash yourself in the stream and I will see if I can wake Anna."

"She's already awake. I don't think I need a bath. I'm not very dirty."

Ela had to try hard not to blurt out that he was filthy. But, remembering that he had been hurt by unkind words in the past, she said, "All good Cherokee braves bathe each morning. It makes them healthier, and the enemy cannot smell them if they are clean."

"I'll be right back," said Johnny as he ran toward the stream. Ela smiled. She would have to remember that trick.

Back at the hut, Anna greeted Ela with, "Today is the day! I just can't wait to leave, but it's so cold, we'll have to move quickly to keep warm. I don't know why winter wants to keep hanging on. I'm tired of it."

Ela laughed and said, "When we're hot and sweaty this summer, we'll wish we could borrow some of this cold weather, won't we?" Anna agreed. "Do you want any help bathing Zephyr?" asked Ela.

"I'm afraid the water and the air are too cold for her," said Anna.

"We can clean her quickly. The warm milk in her stomach will keep her body warm for awhile. I will go with you, if you want me to. Besides, I want you to teach me more English. I remembered everything you taught me last night." Ela recited her few English words.

"That's pretty good. Now, I think I should teach you how to say COLD WATER.

"What does that mean?" asked Ela.

"I'll show you. Follow me to the stream."

The girls walked back to the stream. Johnny ran past them on his way to the hut. His clean little body was dripping with water. Stripped of his filth, he finally looked cute to Ela. "See, Mighty Panther, you are running faster already. The bath has indeed made you stronger," Ela called after him. He didn't stop to respond.

"You convinced Johnny to wash?" Anna asked in disbelief.

"Yes."

"He must like you a lot. He would never do that for me."

At the stream, Anna unwrapped Zephyr's blanket. "This moss is working well. The blanket is still clean. Ela, would you please hold Zephyr a minute while I wash myself?" Ela took the baby from Anna willingly. Then Anna stepped into the stream without taking her clothes off. She pulled her skirt to her knees and tucked the fabric between her legs. She rolled up the sleeves of her shirt and splashed water over her arms. Anna quickly splashed a little water on her face, then returned to Ela with her hands cupped in front of her. Before Ela could say anything, Anna poured a handful of water on Ela's head. "That's what COLD WATER means," laughed Anna.

"Ah, yes, a good English phrase to know," Ela said as she wiped her hair with her hand. She smiled at Anna, "I'll be sure to add that to my list of words. Now, let's see if I have it right." Ela stepped into the creek and kicked water toward Anna, spraying her from head to toe. "This is COLD WATER?"

"Yes, yes. Oh, please stop," giggled Anna.

Ela was glad that she finally felt comfortable enough with Anna to act more like herself instead of feeling self-conscious. Anna was becoming a good friend. "Do you think you can teach me something a little less wet?" Ela asked.

"All right. This is a good place to teach you how to write the words you have learned." Anna picked up a small stick and wrote the word WATER into the mud on the bank of the stream. "Try to copy this word while I wash the baby."

Ela took the stick from Anna and reminded her. "Be sure Zephyr's clothes are off."

"You just practice. I'll take care of my baby." The young mother was already starting to act more confidently with the care of her child. She sang a lullaby to her daughter over the sounds of the infant's squealing protests.

Ela wrote the word WATER several times. It was strange making the shapes of the letters, but not difficult. She was a good artist and often made drawings in the dirt to entertain the small children she cared for in her village.

"Quick, hand me the blanket," Anna called to her. Ela stopped writing and helped to wrap the crying baby in her warm blanket.

"I don't know if I will still be able to remember how this word is written later," Ela sighed.

"That's all right. It took me a long time to learn to write. Now that I think of it, it doesn't make much sense to be teaching you how to write when you know so few English words. Maybe we should just work on speaking English for now."

"I think you're right. We can practice on our walk home. We'll have plenty of time, and it will give us something to do to pass time quickly."

"That's right. I could even teach you some English songs. By learning the songs, you'll learn lots of English words that you are less likely to forget." Ela was developing a new respect for Anna. Anna was not ignorant and she seemed to be a good teacher.

After breakfast, Anna packed the cooking pot and eating bowls into the tow sack. The leftover corn meal mush was scraped into one of the bowls and wrapped in a cloth. Ela wrapped the small supply of dry corn meal and placed it in the sack with the clean cooking pot for Johnny to carry. Anna would be carrying the baby, and Ela would have to carry the blowgun, darts, spear, and fish trap. She tucked the flint stones into her belt to keep them safe. If the weather continued to be this cold, there was a danger of freezing to death if they had no campfire to warm them at night. As long as they kept moving during the daytime, their bodies would create enough heat to keep them warm.

"Let's go!" Ela finally announced, "I'll lead the way." Ela did not feel as confident as she sounded. The others looked to her with blind trust. Ela had reviewed the landmarks for the trip home numerous times, and she hoped her memory was correct. The journey would start from the spot where Johnny had found Ela unconscious in the creek. She led her friends up the steep hill to the path she had been on with the Catawba.

"I hope we don't run into any more Indian warriors," Johnny said.

"We'll have to be very careful," Ela responded. "We must move as silently as we can. If any of us hears a strange noise, we must signal to each other to get off the path and hide."

"I can whistle like a cardinal," Johnny said.

"So can I," Anna added.

"All right. That will be the signal," said Ela.

As they headed down the path, Ela realized that the weather should have been much warmer by now. It was almost mid-day. She looked up into the sky. Clouds were starting to appear in the sky blocking the sun's warmth. She walked a little faster, then, remembering that she must walk slowly enough for the others to keep up with her, she reluctantly eased her pace for awhile. She looked back. Puffs of white vapor escaped from Johnny's mouth as he tried to keep up with Anna and Ela.

Johnny was getting tired. He became irritable and began to complain of hunger. Anna tried to cheer him by singing a song. She repeated the song several times and encouraged Ela and Johnny to join in as they could. That helped for a short time, but finally Ela decided that the boy needed a rest. She wondered how she would be able to encourage Johnny to continue walking after the rest break.

"We have traveled well so far this morning," Ela announced. "We deserve a short break, but we must move again soon or we will get too cold."

"I'm hungry," Johnny whined.

Just then, Zephyr started crying. "You aren't the only one who's hungry," sighed Anna. "This trip is not going to be as easy as I had hoped it might be." Ela silently agreed with a nod of her head.

"You two go ahead and eat. I'm not hungry yet. I'll just sit here," said Ela.

"Ela, do you have any stories you can tell us while I feed the baby? That might help us forget how tired we are."

"Humm. Let me think."

While Ela tried to remember a story her grandmother had told her, Johnny ate some of the mush left over from breakfast. Then he offered the rest to Anna. She ate the mush as though she had been starving until she noticed that Ela and Johnny were staring at her. Anna looked sheepishly back at them. "Ever since I had this baby, I've been hungry all the time. I feel like a mama bear who just woke up from her winter nap and must fill her empty stomach."

"We'll try to find you enough food," Ela reassured Anna. "By the way, that reminds me of a story." Ela leaned back against a tree, closed her eyes and started her story. "This is a story my grandmother told me when I was Johnny's age."

Long ago there was a brave hunter who walked deep into the forest to find food for his family. Suddenly, he saw a big black bear. He set an arrow into his bow and shot the arrow into the bear's shoulder. The bear looked into the hunter's eyes, then turned and started to run away.

The hunter chased after the bear, shooting arrow after arrow into the side of the bear, but nothing seemed to slow the bear down. Suddenly, the bear stopped. He reached around and pulled all the arrows out of his fur. The hunter stood still and watched. Then the bear turned to the hunter.

"You cannot kill me. I am a medicine bear. You may as well stop wasting your precious arrows."

"But I am so very hungry. I must have food soon or I will die," the hunter replied.

"Then come with me to my cave. I have food I will share with you."

The hunter thought this was a trap. This bear might eat me. I must be very careful.

The bear read the hunter's thoughts. "I will not hurt you. Come with me to my home."

The hunter agreed to come. He was so hungry that he was willing to take the chance of being eaten himself.

The black bear led the hunter to a small village of black bears. The bears were having a council meeting. They were discussing the shortage of food that existed in their village. Their leader was a large white bear. The white bear suddenly turned his nose up into the air and sniffed.

"I smell a human. The spirits have brought food to us. We will eat."

But the magical black bear stepped out into the clearing and held his paw up to keep the other bears from attacking the hunter. "Stop. You may not have this human. I have promised him that he will not be harmed."

"Look," said one of the other bears. "The hunter has a bow and arrows. Let us try to use them to catch some food for ourselves."

So the bears all took turns trying to shoot with the bows and arrows, but their claws got caught in the bow string each time and they were unable to hit any target.

The magical bear took the hunter to his cave. It passed through the hunter's mind that the bear might be taking him in there to eat him without having to share with his brother bears.

Again, the bear heard his thoughts. "No. I will not eat you. Come. It is cold. Winter is coming. I have plenty of food that I will share with you." The hunter went into the warm, dark cave. When his eyes adjusted to the light, he could see that the cave was empty except for himself and the bear. He did not see any food.

"Ah, but I do have food, " the bear stated. " I do like this . . ." and the bear rubbed his paws together. Suddenly, his paws were filled with hazel nuts. Then he said, "And then I do like this . . ." and the bear rubbed his paws together again. His paws were filled with blackberries.

Together, the bear and the hunter ate. They became friends and spent many days together. Over time, the hunter grew hair all over his body, which made him look almost like a bear. However, he stood on two feet, whereas the other bears walked on four feet.

Then one day the magical bear said, "Today, hunters will come to kill me. They will take my coat off my body and cut my meat into pieces. Then they will find you and take you home. But before they take you, you must cover my blood with leaves. Then, as you are led away, you must look back to that pile of leaves."

The hunter did not believe the bear. He thought that if someone knows they will be killed, they will try to escape before the murderers come.

But the hunters did come. They came to the bear's cave and immediately shot the bear in the chest with their arrows. Then they saw the hunter. At first they thought he was another bear, but one hunter recognized his old friend. He gave the hairy man clothes to wear as the other hunters skinned the bear and cut his meat into many pieces. A tear ran down the hairy hunter's face. He covered the blood of the black bear with leaves. Then the hunters walked back towards their village, taking the hairy hunter with them. They had not gone far when the hunter looked back to the pile of leaves. There he saw the bear stand up tall. The bear wiped the leaves from his body and ambled back to his cave. The others did not see this, and the hunter did not tell them.

When the hunter returned home, he had become so much like a bear, that he asked his friends to lock him into a dark room where he would not be disturbed for one week. He claimed he would need that much time to lose his bear ways. His friends did as he requested.

As the days went by, the hunter lost much of his body hair. However, on the third day, the hunter's wife came to the little cabin room where he was kept and begged the friends to release her husband. But they would not. She returned the next day. She begged to her husband, screaming through the door, "Come out my husband. I have not seen you in so long that I think I might die if I do not see you." But he would not answer her.

On the fifth day, the woman told her husband's friends that she would set a curse on them if they did not release her husband. "After all," she said, "you can hear that my husband does not answer me when I call to him. He may be very ill. I must see him now."

So the men opened the door to the room in which the hunter sat. He was well, but did not want to return home. When his wife started crying and pleading with him to come home, he sadly went to his cabin. But the hunter had not shed all his bear ways, and as would happen to any bear that was forced to live with humans, the hunter soon died.

"If I was the hunter, I would have returned to the medicine bear and stayed with him forever," said Johnny.

"Wouldn't you miss your family?" Anna asked.

"No. Not me," Johnny claimed. "I would want you and Zephyr to visit me sometimes, but I wouldn't miss anyone else."

"Come," Ela interrupted. "We have rested long enough. I am getting cold. We must walk quickly to keep warm."

Progress was slow as the path wound along a mountain ridge. The view should have been spectacular, but the clouds surrounding the mountains limited vision to objects within a hundred paces. Fortunately, the path was well cleared and there was little chance of getting lost. The best part about following the ridge was that the path stayed at a fairly even level.

Far below the trail, to the left, Ela could hear the sound of water rushing over rocks. It would be out of the way to walk all the way down the mountain to the stream, but Ela felt sure the stream would be teaming with fish at this time of year. The travelers would need a substantial evening meal if they were to have the energy to continue with the journey. So far, Ela had seen no signs of wild game to hunt. It would probably take less time to go down to the stream to fish than it would to hunt. It was also necessary that she and the others have fresh water to drink. So Ela led her friends off the trail and carefully down the steep slope, winding back and forth so that the descent would not be so treacherous.

The river was not as big as Ela had pictured in her mind. It was only the width of her cabin and deep enough to reach to her knees in mid-stream. Trees grew to the water's edge, their branches forming a canopy over the water. Ela set her weapons down and told Johnny to set his pack down.

"We'll have to build a dam across the stream if we want to catch any fish," she told him.

"But the water is so cold," he complained.

"Every young Indian boy knows how to catch fish this way," Ela said. "It's time you learned, too."

So Johnny took his moccasins off, and then he and Ela waded into the icy water while Anna rocked Zephyr in her arms on shore.

When Johnny and Ela had built a wall of rocks across the narrow stream, the water became deeper on the side of the rocks that was upstream and shallower on the downstream side.

"Now, Johnny, I want you to stand upstream. When I tell you to, you need to slap the water with this branch as you walk slowly toward the dam," said Ela as she handed him one from a nearby evergreen.

"But my feet are so cold I can't feel them anymore."

"We're almost done. Can't you help me for just a few more moments?"

"Don't give up now," Anna encouraged her brother.

"I'll try," the young boy responded.

"Good," Ela said. She got the fish trap and placed the open end of it near the center of the stone dam. Then she took out the biggest rock at that point. Doing so allowed the backed up water to rush through the gap. "Now, Johnny, splash as much as you can," she called to him.

Johnny hollered and screamed at the fish as he whipped the water with the branch. He was halfway to Ela when she saw a brook trout flop through the hole in the dam, right into her trap. "We've caught one!" she shouted. "Stop for a moment," Ela called to Johnny. Quickly, she carried the trap to where Anna sat, and she dumped the brook trout out onto the ground. "Take care of our fish," she told Anna. "Don't let him get back into the stream."

"I will," Anna assured Ela. She picked up a nearby rock and knocked the fish in the head. "He won't go anywhere now," she announced.

Ela ran back to the stream and resumed her position near the dam. "Do it again, Johnny. This will be the last time." Soon they captured another brook trout and brought it over to Anna. Johnny cuddled in Anna's arms along with Zephyr to warm himself. Anna wrapped her blanket around both children. Ela killed the second fish with Anna's rock.

"Good work, Mighty Panther," Ela said to Johnny. "You must have a secret for finding the biggest fish in the stream." Johnny smiled with pride. "Stick your feet in my lap. I'll warm them for you," Ela offered. So he stuck a bare foot out from under Anna's blanket. Ela held the foot in both her hands and breathed her warm breath on it. She continued until the little boy said he could feel his foot again. Then she did the same to his other foot.

"Would you like me to do that for you?" Johnny asked Ela. "It feels good."

"No, thank you," she answered. "We must try to walk farther before nightfall." Ela placed both trout in the trap and carried the trap over her shoulder. It took a long time to reach the trail again, but once they did, the walking seemed much easier in comparison to the climb. No one complained again.

As they walked, Ela noticed the air had become very still. The birds were quiet. She looked up into the cloudy sky. As she did, a snowflake landed on her cheek.

At the same moment, Anna called out, "Look! It's snowing. What will we do now?"

Ela was worried, but she tried not to show it. "A little snow won't stop us. We can be glad it's not rain. If it was, our clothes would get drenched. Snow can be brushed off," she explained.

So they walked on. Ela could see that the trail was starting to head downhill. They were probably nearing the end of the ridge. The trail would lead back down to the river. The snowfall became heavier, and the wind started to blow. At a lower elevation, the snow would likely be mixed with rain which would make the cold penetrate their clothing quickly.

"Ela, I think we should go back to our hut. The path is getting slippery. I might fall with the baby," Anna cried.

"But if we go back, we must travel all this distance again," Johnny reminded her.

"Your sister is right. It may be dangerous to travel any farther today, but we can find shelter near here. Up here on the mountain, there should still be plenty of dry sticks we can use to build a fire."

"Then hurry and build a fire before Zephyr freezes," Anna cried with fear in her eyes. Ela looked around. She searched for a large pine tree that would block out the snowfall, leaving a dry spot at its base for the children to spend the night. But there were only oak trees and mountain laurel bushes.

"Ela, the wind is getting too strong for me to keep Zephyr warm. We must find shelter."

"Maybe the medicine bear lives near here, and we can stay with him like the brave hunter did," Johnny suggested.

"Oh, Johnny, don't be such a baby. There is no medicine bear," Anna told her brother.

"Actually, Johnny has a good idea. Maybe there is a cave up there where all the cliffs are," said Ela as she pointed to a wall of rock that jutted up from a nearby hill farther ahead along the trail. "Do you think you can make it that far?" she asked Anna. "I'll carry Zephyr if you'll carry the fish."

"I'll try to carry her for a little while longer," Anna said.

"Good," said Ela. "Everyone, pick up as many dry sticks as you can along the way. We will need them for a fire whether we find a cave or not."

Up they climbed toward the cliff. When they were close, Ela said, "You wait here while I look for a cave. If I find one, I'll call down to you."

"Why can't we come with you," Johnny asked.

"Because if I do find a cave, it may belong to a cougar and I'll have to escape quickly. You might get in the way."

"Then I'll stay here and protect Zephyr and Anna with the blowgun," he said.

"I knew I could count on you," Ela said. Then she stepped off the path and climbed the hill that led to the cliff. She saw many holes and cracks in the surface of the wall of rock, some with seedling trees growing out of them and some with abandoned birds' nests. Ela had to step around bushes that grew at the base of the cliff. At one point, she almost fell down the hillside as she tried to maneuver around a large boulder that partially blocked the narrow walking space. Ela could barely see her friends through the thickly falling snow. There was no cave entrance to be found. Now what would she do? She would have to tell her friends and try to lead them back to the old hut. As she walked back along the narrow path, the large boulder again was in her way. She wrapped her arms around the top of the rock as she passed to keep from falling. She expected to feel her hands rub against the cliff wall as she did so. Instead, the tips of her fingers slipped into emptiness. Ela moved some of the little plants away that grew on the top of the boulder and found there was a huge hole behind the rock. She could feel warm air escaping from the hole. It was a cave. There would be no large animals in this cave because no animal could fit in through the small opening between the boulder and the cave entrance.

Ela knew she didn't have the strength to pull the boulder away, but she tried anyway. Her feet slipped from under her, and she hung from the rock with her feet trying to anchor themselves in the mud. Finally, she found solid ground to the side of the rock with her toe and was able to stand again. An idea popped into her mind. Ela would let the weight of the boulder do the work for her. There was very little ground holding the boulder in position.

"Did you find something?" Anna called up to Ela.

"Yes. I've found a cave, but it's blocked with a boulder. I'm going to try to dig under it so that it will fall down the hill. Come up here near me so you won't get hurt when it falls."

Johnny and Anna quickly joined Ela. They watched as Ela took a large tree branch she had found and sharpened one end with Johnny's knife. Then she jabbed at the earth that lay at the base of the boulder, starting at the hill slope and working towards the boulder. Slowly, chunks of soil broke loose and tumbled down the hillside. Ela worked the landslide closer and closer to the boulder. Finally, as she stabbed at the soil closest to the boulder, the boulder gave a little shudder. "Stand back!" Ela shouted, as she jumped out of the way. Slowly, the massive rock tipped over and rolled down the hill, crashing into smaller rocks, knocking down small trees, and landing with a loud thud against a sturdy oak tree.

"Hooray for Ela," Johnny shouted.

Carefully the children stepped into the cave. A sudden cry echoed though the cave, and the thumping of wings filled the air.

"Bats!" screamed Anna, as she crouched down and leaned forward to shelter Zephyr with her body.

"Ela," cried Johnny. "Save me!"

Ela laughed. "You two act like you've never seen bats before. They won't hurt you. They're scared of you. Look," she pointed out, "they are flying out a small hole in the cave ceiling. The hole will give us light and will make a good chimney for our campfire. Let's build the fire right away."

When the fire was built, the children roasted their fish. They collected piles of snow from the opening of the cave and melted it for warm drinking water. The hot food and drinks warmed their bodies quickly, and soon they were satisfied. Evening had arrived.

Johnny quickly regained his energy. "Let's explore the cave and see how big it is," he suggested.

Ela had not looked very carefully around the cave since she had been so concerned about getting her friends warm and fed. Now that she had a moment, Ela could see they were sitting in a room about twice as large as the hut, but the ceiling was much higher, leading to the hole at the top. The part of the room near the entrance was well lighted by the fire, but the back portions of the cave were still very dark. Ela wondered if there might not be another room in the cave.

"Let's light a stick and see if we can see anything," said Ela. The flame on the stick provided little light. Ela carried it to the darkest area of the room with Johnny following closely behind.

"I'm staying right where I am," Anna announced. "Don't you dare scare any more bats in my direction."

Ela and Johnny laughed and walked on. There was another room, and it was much larger than the other. As they entered the room, Johnny tripped over something. Ela held the flame down to see what had tripped Johnny. It was an old torch. How strange, Ela thought. She picked it up and tried to see if it would light with the flame on her stick. It did. Now they had more light.

"What is that pile over there?" asked Johnny as he pointed to what looked like a small mound of sticks. Ela walked over to the pile with her torch, but when she could see better, she gasped.

"What is it? What is it?" Johnny cried as he tried to see around her back.

"They're bones. Human bones. It looks like the bones of three people," Ela reported. "But how could they have gotten in here?"

Anna came rushing in when she heard the excitement. When she saw the skeletons, she turned away quickly. "How horrible!"

she cried. "I'm not staying here tonight. Their ghosts may still be in the cave."

"We have no choice," Ela reminded Anna. "This is the only safe place for us to be."

"How long do you think those bones have been here?" Johnny asked.

"For a long time. There is no flesh left on the bones."

"Look at the funny clothes the skeletons are wearing," said Johnny as he touched the coat on one of the bodies.

"Don't touch them," Anna warned, but he continued to investigate.

"I've never seen any clothes like those," said Ela. "Have you, Anna?"

Anna put her hands over her face and turned to take a quick look through her fingers at the dead people. Her interest got the better of her, and she took a closer look at the deteriorating fabric. "Those coats look like old-fashioned British suits. See if there are any guns or other things the men may have brought in here." Ela and Johnny searched the small room.

"I found a gun!" Johnny called out. He picked up a pistol and aimed it toward Ela.

"Be careful," Anna shouted. "Don't point that thing at anyone. It could be loaded."

"Aw, don't worry. See? It doesn't work." He aimed the pistol up to the ceiling and pulled the trigger. BAM went the gun. Ela's heart felt like it had stopped. Even her breathing had stopped. She didn't know when she had ever heard such a loud sound. It echoed through the cave chambers. Johnny dropped the gun and started crying, "I'm sorry. I'm sorry."

"Johnny, you could have killed us," Anna yelled. "Don't ever do that again." She grabbed her little brother and dragged him back to the front room of the cave. There Zephyr was crying hysterically from hearing the gun blast.

Ela was left alone in the skeleton room. When her ears stopped ringing, she looked more closely at the skeletons. She felt strongly that the spirits of the dead men were nearby.

"Who are you?" she whispered. "Why are you here in this cave?"

No one answered. No answer ever came when Ela tried to make contact with the Ghost Country, the place where spirits of dead ancestors live. Grandmother often talked to spirits. Calling to the spirits had become like a harmless game to Ela since Grandmother had told her the story of the daughter of the Sun.

The Sun was very angry at the people on earth because they always squinted their eyes when they looked at her, but they smiled when they looked at her brother, the Moon.

The daughter of the Sun lived in the middle of the sky. Every day the Sun went to visit her daughter. Since the Sun was still angry with the earth people, she sent down strong rays of heat that made the people on earth very sick and many died.

The earth people called to their friends, the Little Men, to help them. The Little Men said that to save the earth people, the Sun must be killed. By magic, two of the earth people were turned into snakes. One was a rattlesnake and the other was a copperhead. They wriggled their way to the home of the daughter of the Sun to wait for the Sun to leave her daughter's house. The copperhead was very worried. He was not sure if he was doing the right thing, but the rattlesnake was very excited. He could hardly wait to strike out at the wicked Sun. Soon, the door to the house opened and the rattlesnake attacked his victim, injecting poisonous venom into her leg. But, alas, it was not the Sun. It was the daughter of the Sun who was killed. Quickly, the snakes escaped.

The Sun was so sad at the death of her daughter that she hid in a cave. She left the earth in complete darkness and refused to come out. The people could not live without light, so again, they went to the Little Men for help. They were told that only if they brought the daughter of the Sun back to her mother from the Ghost Country, would the sun shine again. Seven men were chosen to retrieve her body and put it in a wooden box. Each man was given a short sourwood stick. When they went to the Ghost Country, they would see all the ghosts dancing around in a circle. The men were to stand outside the circle and when the girl passed by in the dance, they were to knock her down with their sticks. Then they were to put her in the box and bring her back to her mother, but they must not ever open the box once the girl was put into it.

This is what the men did. Each time the girl passed the men in the dance, one of the men hit her with his stick. The seventh time around, she fell to the ground. The other ghosts didn't seem to notice. The girl was put in the box, but while the men carried her back to her mother, she came back to life. She called from inside the box, "I am hungry. Won't you feed me?" But the men would not answer her, for they were warned not to open the box. When they were near the hiding place of the Sun, the girl cried out weakly. "Please open the lid of this box just a little. I am smothering in here."

The men were afraid she really was dying, so they lifted the lid a little to give her air. As they did, they heard a rush of wind blow through the box and a redbird in a nearby tree cried out. The men shut the box, feeling that the girl had gotten enough air, but when they got the box to the Sun and opened it to reveal her daughter, the box was empty. Then they realized that the redbird was the daughter of the Sun and that they should not have opened the box. If they had followed the instructions of the Little Men, they would have known the secret of how to bring the dead back to life. However, since they had disobeyed, it was never again possible.

The Sun was so sad that her daughter was lost forever, she cried and cried, causing a great flood on the earth. The people were afraid that everyone would drown, so again they went to the Little Men. The people were told to send their most handsome braves and maidens to sing and dance for the Sun to make her happy again. This they did, but all the singing and dancing did not seem to help. The Sun kept crying. The dancing maidens *reminded her of her daughter. Finally, the drummer thought of a funny song to play. He beat on his drum and shouted out the words to his song. The Sun looked up. She had never heard such a song and she could not help but smile. She forgot her grief and decided to shine again.*

Ela returned to the front room of the cave to prepare a place to sleep. Anna, Johnny and the baby were already curled up on the floor around the low-burning fire. Anna was still awake.

"Who do you suppose those people were?" Ela asked.

"I think I know. My father told me that many years ago there were some men from England who came through these mountains to find gold. Apparently, they found some and filled their pockets with the nuggets. As the men were returning to Charles Town with it, a group of Cherokee braves attacked them. The white men were outnumbered, so they scrambled up to a cave for safety. From there, they were able to fire at the Cherokee with their guns. The Cherokee didn't want to waste their arrows or risk losing any of their braves, so they waited patiently until they had a sure target. One by one, each of the Englishmen was killed as he ventured too near the cave entrance. Finally, there was only one Englishman left. He decided to wait until dark to make his escape attempt."

"Did he make it?" Johnny asked.

"I thought you were asleep," Anna said.

"Well, I'm not. Did the man escape?"

"He must have, because somebody had to live to tell the story."

"But how could he have done it?" Johnny asked.

"If it was truly this cave," Ela said, "he may have climbed out the hole in the ceiling. I'm sure a small man could fit through there."

"How did the rock get in front of the doorway?" asked Johnny.

"The Indian braves could have rolled it there to hide the bodies," said Anna. "You know how it is. White people are allowed to kill Indians, but Indians aren't allowed to kill white people."

"I wonder if there is any gold left in the clothes of the skeletons," Johnny said.

"I doubt if the man who escaped would leave any gold in here for the Indians to take," said Anna.

"You're probably right, but I'll check just to make sure." Johnny started to take his blanket off, but Anna said, "Not now. Daylight will be here all too soon. You can look in the morning."

CHAPTER EIGHT

"Ela, where are you?"

Ela sat up quickly. It was Grandmother calling to her. "I'm here, Grandmother," she cried. "Where are you? I can't see you."

Shadows swirled around the cave. Ela's skin prickled as though hundreds of ants were crawling up her arms. She tried to rub the feeling away, but nothing helped.

The voice came again. "Ela, come home."

"I'm trying to, Grandmother."

"I'm trying to . . . trying to," echoed the mocking voices of invisible spirits. Ela hid beneath her blanket and cried for the first time since she had been kidnapped.

"Ela?" whispered a gentle voice. Then Ela felt a tender touch on her shoulder.

"Grandmother?" cried Ela as she pulled the blanket from her face.

"Wake up. Ela. It's me, Anna. Are you all right?"

Ela rubbed the tears from her eyes and looked around the cave again. There were no more strange shadows. The faint light of dawn gave a soft illumination to the cave entrance. Anna looked down on Ela with concern. "You're not sick again, are you?" she asked.

"No. I just had a bad dream. That's all."

"I was afraid the raven might have scared you. It woke me up a few minutes ago with its squawking."

"Little Sister! Where is she?" asked Ela, looking towards the cave entrance.

"She was right there a moment ago," said Anna as she pointed at the cave entrance. "Maybe she flew away when you called out in your sleep. I'm surprised Zephyr didn't wake up."

Ela wrapped her blanket around her shoulders and went to the cave entrance to see if Little Sister was nearby. "Look, Anna," she said. "The snow has stopped. The air is already warmer than it was yesterday." Droplets of melting snow dripped from the trees and ran in tiny rivers down the hillside. Ela wondered why Little Sister should have been looking for her. She wondered if the raven had anything to do with her hearing Grandmother's voice.

Ela told Anna, "The heat from the sun should have all the snow melted from the path soon. We might as well rest until then. We have a lot of walking to do today." Anna agreed and both girls lay back down.

When they woke up later, the sun was already blazing in the sky. Johnny remembered to check the pockets of the clothes on the skeletons. He returned with his hands empty and his head down.

"Are we still poor?" Anna laughed.

"It didn't hurt to look," Johnny responded. "After all, I did find this," said Johnny. He raised his shirt. There he had a leather belt that wrapped twice around his middle. Attached to the belt was a bag. When Ela looked inside the bag, she saw black powder.

"What is this?" she asked.

"It's gunpowder. Remember the gun I found last night? This powder is used to make the pistol shoot. Look at this." He pulled a box out of his pocket. Inside was a metal block about as big as Ela's hand. There were several hollows in the metal.

"What is that thing?" Ela asked again.

"It's a bullet mold. If we had some lead to melt down and mold into bullets, we could use this pistol as our weapon."

"Did you look for any bullets?" asked Anna.

"Yes, but there weren't any. They must have used them all except for the one that was left in the gun."

"Johnny, you better let me or Ela carry that for you. It could be dangerous," said Anna.

"No! No! I found it. It's mine!" Johnny shouted. Zephyr started crying.

"Now look what you have done," said Anna, shaking a pointing finger at her little brother. "I'm tired of trying to stop her crying when it isn't my fault that she's upset. Why don't you try to take care of her for awhile?"

Ela lifted the infant into her arms and said to Anna, "We'll both help you with Zephyr if that's what you want. Just tell us what you need. I think Mighty Panther has been very good and has shown us that he can act like an Indian brave when necessary. I trust him to carry the pistol and gunpowder. Without bullets, I don't think there is much danger, is there?"

"I guess not," Anna responded. "Shouldn't we leave here soon? We're wasting precious daylight the longer we sit here talking."

"Yes," said Ela.

They melted snow in a pot over the campfire to wash themselves, and then they ate mush again for breakfast. Soon, the four were back out on the trail. Ela stayed close to Anna's side while walking down the mountain ridge to help keep Anna from falling with Zephyr in her arms. Johnny ran ahead to scout the trail. He took the blowgun with him. Every few minutes he would trot back to the girls to tell them that the way was clear. "No enemy in sight," he would announce. While he was gone, the girls talked.

"Anna," said Ela, "I've never been allowed to help at the birthing hut in my village. I've been wondering what it's like to give birth to a baby. I've heard cries coming from the hut and it makes me worry that having a baby is terribly painful."

"I know how you feel, Ela. I was very frightened about that too when I was your age. I asked my mother about it and do you know what she told me?" Ela shook her head no. "She said, 'Look around you. Count how many women you see that have many children and are still happy and healthy. Do you think that they would have more than one child if the experience was too horrible?'"

"I see her point, but what was it like for you?" Ela asked.

"I was actually relieved when my labor started. The last moon of pregnancy is very uncomfortable. I bumped into everything with my stomach. The baby kicked so much inside of me that it was difficult to rest. There was no comfortable position to sleep in with such a huge belly in front of me. I longed to be able to sleep on my stomach again, so when labor began, I was glad to see the time had come."

"What did labor feel like?" Ela asked as she and Anna plodded along the muddy trail, pushing branches away that blocked their way.

"Do you ever get cramping in your belly when you have eaten unripe fruit?"

"Yes, and it hurts."

"That's what the cramping feels like in labor, but it doesn't last forever," said Anna.

"Would you ever want to have another baby?" Ela asked Anna.

"Not for a long time. It's not easy taking care of a baby. I love Zephyr, but she is a big responsibility. She is with me day and night. I get no time for myself."

Ela was silent over the next few minutes. She was trying to picture herself in Anna's place. "Some day I might not mind devoting a lot of time to my own baby, but for now, there are too many other things I want to do with my life."

"I don't blame you," said Anna.

All of a sudden, Ela realized that she had not seen Johnny for a while. Maybe he had found a wild animal and was stalking it. She decided not to call out to him because it might scare his prey away. After traveling another mile, Ela recognized the charred remains of a burnt section of forest. It was one of the landmarks directing Ela to leave this trail and follow another narrower trail which led to a small mountain. On the other side of the mountain was the Cullasaja River.

Ela stopped Anna. "We need to find Johnny right away. This is our turn."

Anna called out loudly to her brother, but there was no answer. She called again. The forest just absorbed the sound, returning only silence. "Do you think he's lost?" Anna asked Ela with fear in her eyes.

"I don't know how he could be. The path is very clearly marked." A frightened look came over both girls and they started to hurry along the path, each afraid to share her worst fears. Suddenly, they heard a loud cry echo through the trees.

"Johnny!" screamed Anna. She started to run, but the path was instantly blocked by Little Sister. The bird screeched and flapped her wings at the girls. It had been Little Sister's cry that they had heard, not Johnny's.

"Get out of my way, bird," ordered Anna as she tried to get past, but Little Sister jumped up and down, flapping her wings, trying to scare Anna away from the path. "What's wrong with this bird?" Anna asked Ela.

Ela put her finger to her lips to signal to Anna to keep very quiet. Then she squatted down so she could be closer to Little Sister's level. She spoke softly to her friend, "Is something wrong, Little Sister? Are you hurt?" Little Sister stopped flapping her wings. She paced back and forth across the path, giving no answer to Ela.

"This is just wasting time, Ela," said Anna impatiently. "Let's go." Anna stepped forward to search for her brother. Immediately, Little Sister started batting her wings again and tried to block Anna's way.

"I think Little Sister is trying to tell us that there is danger ahead. She's afraid we will get hurt."

"Then Johnny must be in danger," said Anna. Panic was rising in her voice.

"Follow me and do as I do," instructed Ela. She moved in slow motion off the path, around the raven, following closely to the path but out of view of any traveler who might be on the path. Her steps were almost silent. Anna was not as skilled in walking silently, but she did her best. Little Sister did not object to their passage as long as the girls were quiet. Then the bird flew away.

For a moment, Ela thought she heard a faint sound far away. She crouched and listened, waving to Anna to do the same. The sound came again a few minutes later. "Horses," Ela whispered to Anna.

"That must mean someone is coming along the path. Maybe they have Johnny. We must hurry to help him." Anna rushed noisily toward the sound of the horses.

Ela easily caught up to Anna and grabbed her around the waist. "Stop. We can't help Johnny that way. The worst thing we could do is to get captured ourselves. The strangers would realize that a young boy like Johnny would not be traveling alone. They are probably waiting for us."

"Johnny would never tell them where we are. Our parents taught us that if we were ever captured by Indians, we must never reveal where other family members are hiding."

"That doesn't matter. All they have to do is wait for us to come after Johnny. I'll go ahead and see if I can find Johnny without getting caught. The baby might start crying if you come with me. Then we would certainly be captured." Ela found a wide spreading pine tree for Anna and Zephyr to hide under. The thick branches would muffle baby sounds and the ground was still dry at the tree's base.

"You two, stay here," Ela ordered the older girl. "If Johnny and I don't come back, walk back to the charred trees we just passed. Follow the narrow path over the mountain. To the west is the river that leads to my village. Someone there will take you home."

"I want to go with you," Anna cried.

Ela firmly insisted that Anna remain. "Just do what you can to keep the baby quiet."

The wet leaves padded Ela's footsteps as she walked toe-heel, toe-heel like a hunter. She planned to circle around to the other side of where she determined the enemy might be. That way she would be able to come up behind them, unnoticed, and evaluate the situation. She hoped that Johnny was still alive.

The dripping water from wet tree branches soaked through Ela's blanket. She tried to avoid sunlit rocks and logs upon which rattlesnakes and copperheads loved to sun themselves at that time of year.

There had been no sounds of horses for several minutes. Ela walked much farther than she had estimated she would need to. Then she aimed back toward the sound of the creek where she knew she would find the path. There were no leaves on the trees, so it was easier for Ela to watch for the enemy, but unfortunately, it also made it easier for her to be seen in return. As she neared the path, she crouched low and darted from tree to tree, working her way back to where Johnny and the enemy must be. She wondered how many men there were and what weapons they might have. Johnny had her blowgun, so all Ela had for her own defense was Johnny's little knife. Her best course of action would be to outsmart the enemy.

As she came around a bend in the stream, she saw the soil on the path had been churned up where there might recently have been the kicking of horses' feet or those of men. This must be where Johnny was captured. He must have put up quite a struggle. Ela inched forward, and there, over a small hill, she saw Johnny. He was alive and tied to a tree. His mouth was gagged. No wonder he hadn't given his cardinal whistle to warn the girls of danger. His blowgun was on the ground near the tree.

A young white man stood near Johnny, but he was not watching the boy. He was looking up the path to where his companions had probably ventured while he had been left behind to guard the prisoner and the horses. Three ponies were loosely tied to a nearby tree, their heads reaching down to eat the grass the young man had gathered for them to keep them quiet. He appeared to be a hunter, for he was wearing a buckskin shirt and pants. A few fresh skins of red foxes hung from his belt. It was unusual for white hunters to enter the mountains unless game was scarce in their land to the east.

Ela wondered why the man had made Johnny a prisoner. The boy was part white. Then she realized that Johnny looked almost pure Indian. Since he was gagged, he could not speak English to the men and explain their mistake.

Johnny had not seen her yet. He held his head up high, looking with hatred at his enemy. Ela crept forward and made her way behind the thick tree trunk to which Johnny was tied. Quickly, she wrapped her arms around him so that he could not struggle with surprise. Ela looked Johnny in the eyes and whispered in his ear, "Don't worry. I'm here to help you. I'm going to hide over in the bushes while I think of a plan. Be very quiet."

She hid behind a wild rhododendron bush whose thick green leaves provided good cover. She was tempted to cut Johnny's bindings with the knife, but it would make a sawing noise and the guard could hear. Just then, Ela could see the guard walk over and sit near Johnny. If she tried to stab the guard, there was the chance he would not be killed instantly, allowing him to call out to his friends, or even to turn around and kill Ela.

Another idea occurred to Ela. What if she started a fire just close enough to the guard that he would notice the smoke, but far enough away that he would have to leave Johnny to check it out?

Ela stood up quickly and checked her supplies. She found the flint in her belt together with a few blowgun darts. The cotton from the darts were still dry and would be good kindling for the fire. She searched under the thickest bushes to locate dry leaves and sticks. After some time she was able to gather a small arm load of material with which she could build a small fire.

Ela lifted her face to the breeze that blew through her hair. She judged its direction and then walked to a spot upwind from where the guard stood. She lit a small fire and, once it was burning well, she threw some moist leaves at the base of the fire. Smoke billowed into the air. The breeze picked it up and blew it toward the guard. Ela quickly returned to her rhododendron to wait.

The guard kept his eyes on the path where his companions must have been hiding. Ela could see the smoke drifting about the guard, but he didn't seem to notice. Ela picked up a rock and threw it as hard as she could toward the direction of the fire.

Immediately, the guard looked toward the sound. He seemed to hesitate in following his instinct to investigate. Maybe he feared punishment from his companions. Then a smoke cloud blew right into his face. This caused him to start coughing. Even Johnny was coughing. The guard looked up and down the path and then at Johnny. Finally, the white man gave in and jogged off toward the source of the smoke.

The moment the guard entered the woods, Ela hurried to untie Johnny from the tree. She left the gag in his mouth so he couldn't make any unnecessary noise. Then she grabbed his hand and the blowgun, and they both ran as quietly as possible back to Anna's hiding place.

When she saw her little brother, Anna started crying with relief. She rushed out from under the tree to hug him. Zephyr was pressed between the two and began to cry. Johnny pointed anxiously at his gag, so Anna untied it.

The moment it was off, Johnny said, "Ela saved me."

"What happened?" Anna demanded to know.

"Three white men attacked me and tied me to a tree. They were going to catch you, too. You should have seen Ela trick my guard by starting a fire. When he ran to put it out, Ela rescued me."

Anna gave Ela a big hug. "How can I ever thank you enough?"

"You can both thank me by moving as quickly as possible. We must get far away from here. Come," she said. She led her friends away from the stream and down the narrow path. Once they were over the mountain crest, Ela felt safe. There, below her, flowed the Cullasaja.

"At last, I'm near home and soon you will be home, too," said Ela.

"But I want to stay with you," Johnny said to Ela.

"We'll talk about that later," said Ela. Then she pointed to the river. "We'll stop down there to rest and eat, but then we must continue walking until it grows dark."

By the time the group arrived at their destination, they were exhausted. Johnny fell asleep moments after he finished his bowl of corn meal. The girls decided to let him sleep for a while so that he would have enough energy to hike for the rest of the afternoon. The girls lay down to rest, placing the sleeping Zephyr between them.

Anna sighed, "When I get home, I'm going to roast a turkey and bake a big loaf of bread. Then I am going to eat it all myself."

Ela laughed. "It will be good to be home. I never realized how nice it was to be able to tend to the village children and work in the fields and play with my friends without having any fears."

"You haven't seemed frightened to me," said Anna. "You were very brave when you rescued Johnny. You've guided us through the mountains safely. It seems to me that you don't need anybody to take care of you." It felt good to be admired by Anna. Ela hoped Anna was right. There were still many miles to travel before they reached home.

Soon it was time to wake Johnny. They walked until the shadows from the mountains shaded the river valley, warning the travelers that evening was rapidly approaching. Ela hoped to have enough light to catch fresh fish for dinner and set up a campsite. She chose a spot on the opposite bank of the river from where the path lay. That way strangers could be seen who might be traveling along the path, thus giving the young people time to hide before the strangers could see them. Ela wanted no more surprise encounters.

Fishing would be more difficult on the Cullasaja than the last river where they had fished because the Cullasaja was much wider, and building a dam would not be practical. Ela took the spear she had made and stood patiently on a rock near a pool of water where the river current was weak. After a long wait, Ela spied a long, shining fish hiding among the rocks.

Without wasting a moment, Ela threw her spear. The fish was hit. It tried to swim to safety, but the spear made of cane was too buoyant to allow this. Ela was able to grab the spear and pull the fish out of the water. She brought her catch back to the campsite.

Ela and Johnny built a small fire with a foot-high wall of rocks around the side facing the river to keep the fire from being seen by strangers. Suddenly, Ela heard a strange bird song. Anna and Johnny lifted their heads up from their meals to listen, too. "I've never heard a bird like that before. Do you know what kind it is?" Ela asked Anna.

Anna quickly stood up with a fearful expression on her face. "That's not a bird. That's a flute."

The sound came closer. Although it was a beautiful sound, Ela knew it meant that strangers were approaching again.

"Quick, put out the fire," she ordered as she tried to force her eyes to see any movement on the other side of the river. Johnny threw dirt on the fire and huddled close to Ela. It was then that Zephyr started to cry.

CHAPTER NINE

The flute music stopped instantly.

"Make the baby stop crying!" Ela ordered Anna in a loud whisper. Anna tried bouncing and patting Zephyr, but she was so nervous, her forceful movements only made Zephyr cry louder.

A shout came from across the river. It was a male voice speaking in a language Ela could not understand. She wondered if the white hunters had trailed them to this spot. "What is he saying?" she asked Anna.

"I don't know," cried Anna. Then, looking down at Zephyr, she pleaded, "Please be quiet. You'll get us all killed."

Johnny stood and tried to run away, but Anna grabbed him with her free hand. "Where are you going? Stay here or you'll get lost."

"I'm not staying around here. Whoever is over there knows we're here because of that noisy baby. I don't want to be captured again," he announced.

Before Anna could respond, the man's voice called out again, this time in a language that sounded very different from the first. They still could not understand what he was saying.

"What are we going to do?" Anna asked Ela as she held on to both Zephyr and Johnny.

"We could try to sneak away together, but it's too dark to see where we're going."

"As long as Zephyr is with us, we'll be found," Johnny pointed out.

Then the flute playing started again. Zephyr stopped crying, her attention drawn to the music. The tune being played was slow and peaceful, entrancing even Johnny and Anna. Ela thought of a spider spinning its beautiful web to attract insects that would later be devoured.

"What do you think he wants?" Anna asked. "He couldn't be too dangerous if he can play such beautiful music."

Without asking permission, Johnny shouted out to the man in English, "MY SISTER WANTS TO KNOW WHAT YOU WANT."

"AH, YOU SPEAK ENGLISH!" the man responded with a thick German accent. "I WANT NOTHING. I JUST THOUGHT YOU MIGHT NEED SOME HELP. I HEARD THE BABY CRYING."

"Be quiet," Ela ordered Johnny with a loud whisper. "He may be trying to figure out how many of us are over here." Then she asked Anna what the man had said. Anna translated.

"I don' t think we need to worry. One man can't hurt all of three of us. We outnumber him," Anna said.

"How do we know there is only one man over there?" Ela responded. "It's too dark to tell."

The man continued, "MY NAME IS CHRISTIAN PRIBER. I WILL NOT HURT YOU." Anna translated the words to Ela.

"Tell him to stay where he is or we'll have our warriors cross the river and pierce him with arrows," Ela ordered Anna.

Anna chuckled, but shouted out the message to the man. He called back, "I WILL STAY RIGHT WHERE I AM FOR THE NIGHT, AND YOU CAN STAY OVER THERE. HOWEVER, I HAVE SOME FOOD OVER HERE I WOULD BE HAPPY TO SHARE WITH YOU AND YOUR WARRIORS."

When Anna translated, Ela told her to tell him they would not share food with a stranger. Anna did as she was told. No further words were exchanged.

The young people huddled together as they listened to the man moving about over the crackling leaves and twigs on the opposite bank of the river. Soon the spot was illuminated by a single campfire, and they could see the shadowed outline of a short, stocky man. He wore a blanket around his shoulders. Casually he prepared his evening meal.

"See, Ela, there's only one man."

"I'm still hungry," whined Johnny, "and my hands and feet are freezing. Can't we build a fire, too?"

"I'm not sure," said Ela. "Let me think."

"We'll have to start a fire to keep Zephyr warm, Ela," said Anna.

"I know, but I still don't trust that man. There may be others in the shadows that we can't see. Maybe we can build a few campfires so it seems that there are other people with us."

"Good!" said Johnny. "Then we can finish eating."

Ela built three fires. Two were constructed behind trees so that the stranger would have no clear view of how many people were sitting around the campfires. The other one she rekindled from the one Johnny had put out earlier. They finished cooking their fish and ate hungrily. The night air was cold but the water on the ground was not freezing yet, so there was a good chance the night would not become dangerously cold.

"How much farther is it until we get to your village?" Anna asked Ela.

"One day's journey. We could arrive before nightfall if we get an early start and walk quickly,"

"Tell us another story, Ela," Johnny said.

"Oh, Johnny, I have too many things on my mind to tell you a story."

Johnny did not answer. Then Ela heard a few little sniffles. "Johnny, don't cry. I'm just tired. We should go to sleep."

"I'm too cold to sleep," he cried.

Ela pulled him close to her, wrapping him in her blanket. The warmth from his small body plus the heat from the campfire stopped her shivering. Anna cradled Zephyr in her arms and scooted as close to Ela as she could get. The flute music resumed, lulling the mother and infant to sleep. Ela felt they would be safe as long as the music did not sound any closer. She wished she could make such beautiful music. She loved to sing, but she was often teased by the other children in the village. They said her voice was too squeaky, so Ela rarely tried to sing in public.

"Please, Ela. Tell me a story, even if it is just a little one," Johnny pleaded.

"Well, all right. Just a short story. But then you have to go right to sleep." Johnny settled down into a more comfortable position and waited.

A long time ago, the Turtle had the most beautiful whistle in the forest. Now, you may tell me that the Turtle makes no sound, but long ago he was able to whistle lovely tunes. One day the Partridge became envious of the Turtle, for the Partridge, back then, had no whistle.

"Turtle," the Partridge said, "Will you please let me borrow your whistle?"

"No," he responded. "For you will steal it from me and never give it back."

"I promise I won't," said the Partridge. "If you want to, you can stay right here with me while I try playing it."

The Turtle gave in and let the Partridge play with his whistle, but he kept close to the Partridge as the bird strutted about whistling a little tune that he composed as he played.

"How am I doing?" asked the Partridge as he started playing faster and walking more quickly ahead of the Turtle.

"That is very good for a beginner," the Turtle said as he tried to keep up with the Partridge.

The Partridge speeded up, calling behind him, "How do you like this tune?" as he played a little faster.

"You are doing very well," the Turtle panted, "but you will have to slow down. I can't keep up with you."

But instead of slowing down, the Partridge spread his wings and flew up to the top of a nearby tree, and played mockingly on the whistle.

The poor Turtle waited for hours but the Partridge would not return the whistle. And for all these years, the Partridge has kept the whistle. And since then, the Turtle has been unable to make a sound. He has been so embarrassed for being tricked that he hides himself inside his shell whenever anyone comes near him even to this day.

"I liked that story," Johnny said sleepily. "Good night."

"Good night, Mighty Panther," Ela whispered. Then she closed her eyes. But she did not fall asleep for a long while. She was straining her ears, listening for any sounds that could mean the stranger was approaching, but all she heard was the hooting of owls. The weather was not warm enough for insects to be noisy, and there was no croaking of frogs or toads, for they had not emerged from their winter hibernation. The embers of the camp-fire crackled every once in a while. Hoping she wasn't making a mistake, Ela allowed herself to believe that it might be safe enough to sleep.

Much too quickly, the early morning light glowed through Ela's eyelids, urging them to open. The music of the flute was still dancing in her ears like a dream. She sat up and rubbed the sleep out of her eyes. Remembering the stranger, she crawled over to a nearby bush and peeked through its branches to the man across the river who was sitting in the sunlight. He was a strange-looking white man, wearing his blanket around his shoulders, leaving only his face and legs exposed. Ela had never seen skin as white as his. His hair was light brown and grew a strange pattern. There was no hair on the top of his scalp, yet it grew thickly above his ears, around the back of his head, and over his chin. No man in Ela's tribe let hair grow on his face. She thought of how frustrating it would be for the warriors of her tribe not to be able to claim a scalp from this stranger.

Anna came up behind Ela and tapped her on the shoulder. She pointed to the man, "See, I told you he was alone. We didn't have to worry after all."

Suddenly, the man turned and met Ela's gaze with his own even though she was mostly hidden by the bush. How had he known she was watching him?

"HELLO THERE!" Anna called out, waking up Johnny and Zephyr in the process.

"HELLO BACK TO YOU," the man responded. He made no attempt to come toward them. Ela watched him carefully.

"I LIKE YOUR MUSIC," Anna offered.

"THANK YOU," he answered. Then he pointed to Ela, "WHO IS YOUR SHY LITTLE FRIEND?"

"HER NAME IS ELA."

Hearing her own name, Ela ducked further behind the bush. "What did he say? What did he say?" she demanded as she realized they were talking about her. Anna quickly explained.

"HELLO, ELA," Priber called.

Ela felt foolish hiding, but if she stood up now and said hello, he would see her embarrassment, and she would be even more humiliated.

"ELA DOESN'T SPEAK MUCH ENGLISH YET," Anna explained to the man. "I'VE JUST STARTED TEACHING IT TO HER."

"WHAT LANGUAGE DOES SHE SPEAK?" he asked.

"CHEROKEE," Johnny shouted. "MY NAME IS MIGHTY PANTHER."

"NO, IT'S NOT," Anna chided her brother. "HIS NAME IS REALLY JOHNNY."

Priber tried to speak a Cherokee greeting to Ela, but his pronunciations were so bad Ela had to laugh. He laughed at himself and then said in Cherokee, "I understand Cherokee much better than I speak it, but I am willing to try to speak it so that you can understand me."

Ela decided to risk being laughed at, realizing she couldn't sound any sillier than this white man. She stood up, brushed her clothes off, and tried to look dignified. She was glad the man hadn't asked where all of her warriors were that she had threatened him with the night before.

"Would you children like to share my breakfast with me?" he asked in Cherokee. Ela was very hungry and she knew her friends must be, too.

"Let's go," Anna urged Ela. "He seems to be very nice."

"Well, all right. But tell him he should come over to this side of the river and that there are warriors who travel on that path. They wouldn't think twice about killing him if we asked them to."

Anna giggled and then told Priber Ela's message.

"That's a good idea. Thank you," he responded. The man took off his shoes and held them in one of his hands along with his cooking pot that contained the breakfast. He let his blanket drop to the ground as he prepared to cross the river.

"Oh, my goodness, look at the way that white man is dressed," Anna pointed. Priber was wearing a loin cloth over his private parts and that was all. Neither Anna nor Ela had ever seen a white man dressed as an Indian brave.

"Look," cried Johnny. "He is playing Indian just like I do."

"Yes, but he is a grown man," Anna laughed.

When he reached the other side, Priber immediately built another fire to warm water for tea while the young travelers tried some of the hot mush. Johnny offered to help find sticks for Priber's fire, and Anna brought the man water from the stream for the tea. Ela sat on a rock, away from the others, and watched. Her heart beat fast with anger as she picked up a twig from the ground and broke it into pieces, eyeing Priber all the while. *I don't like that man*, she thought. *See how he has taken control of us without being asked.* Priber brought a bowl of mush over to Ela. "I'm not hungry," she said in Cherokee. She hoped he would have trouble understanding her.

Priber could not help seeing the anger in Ela's eyes. "What's wrong?" he asked.

"We don't need your help. We were doing fine without you."

He paused and looked kindly into Ela's eyes. "Yes, I can see you children are safe and healthy." With a tone of understanding, he said, "Have you been taking care of the others?"

"Yes," Ela snapped, surprised at herself for speaking to an adult so rudely, but Priber didn't seem to mind. Not long ago, she had wished an adult would rescue her and take her home. However, since she had started taking on that responsibility herself, she didn't want to give up her independence. "I made our weapons, rescued Johnny from the enemy warriors, and guided Johnny, Anna, and Zephyr through the mountains."

Priber sat down next to Ela, not too close to make her uncomfortable, but close enough so she felt he cared. "You have done a very good job. I won't try to take over your leadership. I'm sorry if it seems that I have. As a matter of fact, I need your help more than you need mine."

Ela turned to him in disbelief. "What could you want from me?"

"I am on the greatest adventure of my life, an adventure for which I have been preparing for over twenty years. It is my hope that you will lead me into your village and introduce me to your leaders, for I have a plan that could help to save the Cherokee Nation."

Anger stirred in Ela's veins again. "We have a mighty nation. We don't need your help, just like I don't need your help now."

"I know your nation has great power, but I have much I can teach your people about how to work with white men so they won't take advantage of you. There will always be thousands of white men trying to steal your land. There are too many white people for the Cherokee to keep away unless your people understand how the white man thinks. Only then can the Cherokee hold some power over him.

"Why would you want to help us?" Ela asked.

"It seems to be the right thing to do — to save a noble nation from destruction. I have many other ideas that I want to discuss with your leaders."

"Our leaders would never trust you," Ela stated.

"That is why I need your help. Your village might accept me if they know that I'm your friend."

"But I'm not your friend."

"Not yet, but you can see I mean you no harm. I have no weapons. I've shared my music and food with you. Maybe, if you give me some time, you will see that I can be a trusted friend. Will you take me to your village?"

"I don't see how I can stop you. That's where I'm going whether you come or not. If you come, I will be watching you closely. The village elders can decide what to do with you when we get there."

"Wonderful," Priber said. He held out the bowl of food again, "Now, it's up to you whether you want to eat or not, but I don't have much food left in my satchel. It might be wise to eat while there is still some left." He handed her the bowl of mush and went away to sit with the others, leaving Ela alone.

Ela stared at the food and her stomach started growling un-controllably. Agitated at her own weakness, she turned her back to the others and ate the hot food quickly. Then she stood up and walked over to Anna and Johnny, ready to take charge again.

"Johnny, you wash with me at the river. Anna, get all our gear together. I'll take Zephyr with me. Then you can wash off quickly when we are ready to break camp."

Anna and Johnny looked surprised at Ela's orders. They turned to Priber for guidance, but he did not return their look. He said to Ela with a smile, "What can I do to help?"

Ela hesitated. She had never given orders to an adult before. Composing herself she said, "You can clean the cooking pot and dishes." Priber, Anna, and Johnny did as they were instructed.

Soon the group was on their way again. They crossed the river to retrieve Priber's belongings. He had a small traveling trunk that was about the size of Johnny. Priber hoisted the trunk up onto his back, which forced him to walk in a stooping position.

"What's in the trunk?" Johnny asked.

"Books, paper and ink," Priber responded.

"What are you going to do with them?" Anna asked.

"I am going to teach the Indians how to read and write, if Ela will help me."

"Are you going to help him, Ela?" Anna asked. "I think you should. You'll love knowing how to read."

Ela did not respond to the question. Instead, she said to Priber, "I hope you don't slow us down too much carrying that heavy load."

"If I can't keep up with you, I give you permission to leave me behind," he responded.

"I'll help you if you need me to," Johnny offered.

"Thank you. I've carried this box for two hundred miles. I think I can make it a bit farther."

As they walked, Anna kept a conversation going. First, she told Priber all about Johnny's and her kidnapping, about finding Ela, and all that had happened since. Then, she started asking him question after question about himself.

"Where are you from?"

"I'm from Germany. Have you heard of it?"

"Oh, yes. I have a book at home with a map of Europe," Anna said.

Ela didn't know what Germany was and didn't care to show her ignorance by asking, so she remained quiet and listened to the others.

"How long have you been in America?" Johnny asked.

"For a few years. I have been living in Charles Town, South Carolina."

"What kind of work do you do?" Anna asked.

"I'm a lawyer, or at least I was in Germany. Since coming to America, I have spent my time trying to persuade people in Georgia and South Carolina to support my efforts to create a new nation within the Americas. I want a place where white people who have been persecuted for minor crimes and native people could come to live in peace. All the citizens of this paradise would share all that they have with one another and all would have to work to help support the nation."

Ela couldn't keep quiet any longer. "We Cherokee already have our own nation. We share everything and work hard. It sounds like you want to have what we already have."

Johnny said, "My father told me that white men will soon have all of the Indian land. He said that I should be proud of the way poor white people, like him, left England and came to America where they have started farms on their own land. He said there will be plenty of land for me when I grow up because this is such a big country."

Ela felt panicky because this was the first time she had heard of the possibility that the Cherokee Nation could lose all their land. Priber and Johnny's father seemed to be aware of a secret plot to destroy her people. Maybe she should lead this group of relative strangers away from her village instead of toward it. What should she do? She finally decided that if she brought Priber to her village, the elders could question him and find out more about the plot. Then they could kill him. Yes, that was what she would do. She would pretend she wasn't worried so that he would not suspect her plan.

Anna continued to question Priber while they walked. "How did you learn the Cherokee language?"

"While I was in Charles Town, I hired a Cherokee man to teach me. He helped me for several weeks. I tried to write down as many of the useful Cherokee phrases that I could, but it was very difficult to write the language with our alphabet. I'm hoping to learn much more of the language."

"I wish I could learn more about the world," Anna sighed.

"Are you planning to stay in Ela's village for long? Maybe I could teach you from some of the books I have in my trunk."

"Oh, I wish I could, but Johnny and I need to return home as soon as possible. I need to see if my parents are all right, and I've got to get home before my husband decides to marry someone else. I'm sure they all think Johnny and I are dead."

"I'm not going home," Johnny informed Priber. "I'm going to be a Cherokee warrior."

"Why do you want to be a Cherokee warrior?" Priber asked.

"Because then I can shoot a bow and arrow and I won't have to work on the farm."

"Can't you shoot a bow and arrow at home?" he asked.

"Well, sometimes I can, but most of the time I'm too darn busy helping my mother pull weeds from the garden."

"I don't blame you for wanting to live with the Cherokee. How wonderful it must be to live so close to nature."

Ela wondered what the man was talking about. He was using words that she wasn't even sure were real Cherokee words. Why couldn't Johnny and Priber be happy with who they were instead of trying to be full-blooded Indians.

"Johnny," Anna said with exasperation in her voice, "Mother will be furious with me if I don't bring you home. Father would hunt you down and drag you home."

"I don't care," Johnny cried. "I'm tired of being teased by the other children in the settlement. They call me a half-breed and say that Mother is a savage. I want to live where people are glad that I'm part Cherokee."

"The children in our village might tease you, too," said Ela. "We haven't had any half-breed children live in our village before."

"I hate all of you," Johnny cried. He sobbed as he continued walking, and he wouldn't accept any attempts at comforting him. Ela hoped Johnny wouldn't create a big scene when they arrived in the village. He needed to go home with Anna and that was that.

The animals in the forest seemed to be quieter than usual. It was likely that the noise of the travelers had frightened them into silence. Only one bird could be heard. Ela couldn't mistake the insistent croaking of her raven. When she looked up, she saw Little Sister hopping from tree top to tree top, trying to keep pace with Ela.

Ela spoke quietly to the bird so as not to draw the attention of Priber. "So, Little Sister, have you come to warn me again of danger? Can you tell me if Priber is good or evil?" Little Sister just continued following Ela. The raven's crowing didn't sound agitated this time, but more like a toddler babbling happily to itself.

"Are you coming back to my village with me to be my pet?" Ela asked. She hoped so. Little Sister would be a reminder of her difficult adventure.

Johnny finally stopped crying. He whined, "Let's have something to eat soon, Ela."

"Not yet," Ela responded. "We should walk until the sun is directly overhead before we eat. Then, we won't have to stop again before we reach my village."

"But I'm hungry now," he complained.

Priber broke in, "Johnny, Ela knows best about this. Try to think of something else until it's time to eat." Ela wished the man would stop being so nice.

"What am I supposed to think about?" Johnny asked.

"Let's sing. You can teach me some of your favorite songs," Priber suggested.

Johnny liked the idea. However, the young boy did not want to sing alone, so he told Anna the song he wanted. She started singing, and Johnny joined in after she had sung it once through. Priber was ready to join in on the third repetition of the song. The three carried on like that for song after song. Ela didn't sing, but she was learning the songs even though she didn't know what the words meant. Finally, Johnny suggested a Cherokee song that his mother had often sung to him. It was a favorite of Ela's. The song made her so homesick that she was tempted to run the rest of the way home.

When the sun was overhead, Ela announced that it was time for the rest break. There was not much food left. Hunting or fishing would take too much time, so they had to make do with small rations. Plenty of food would be waiting for them in Nequassee.

As she ate, Ela heard a rustling of leaves in the distance. No one else seemed to hear, so she decided it was just the wind blowing the leaves. Little Sister squawked a few times, but settled down when Ela threw some of her precious corn meal out on the ground for the raven to eat.

"What a smart bird," Priber commented. "You have certainly trained her well."

"I didn't train her," Ela said.

"Ela, tell Priber about how Little Sister has been following you and how she warned us of the enemy," Anna insisted.

Ela sighed, hoping to sound like this would be a great effort on her part to tell the story. In reality, Ela enjoyed telling Priber about her friendship with Little Sister.

Suddenly, she heard the rustling in the forest again, but this time it was much closer and louder. Little Sister screamed and flew up into a tree just as Ela and the others were surrounded by five Indians pointing arrows directly at them.

CHAPTER TEN

"Don't move," Priber warned his companions. The warning wasn't necessary because fear paralyzed each of them.

Then it occurred to Ela that these men wore their hair like Cherokee warriors. Each had shaved his head except for a small area at the crown of his scalp. There the hair grew long and each man had tied feathers to his top knot of hair. These warriors were not from her village, otherwise she would have known them, but they might be from a neighboring village. She asked the men, "Why are you doing this? I'm a Cherokee."

"Not all of you are Cherokee. Why do you bring the strangers to our land?" asked the leader of the men.

"I am Ela of the Nequassee village. I am trying to return to my home. My father is Awahili. These people are my friends."

One of the younger men said to his leader, "I know Awahili."

"This is Johnny, Anna, and Zephyr. They were kidnapped by the Tuscarora. I am helping them to return to their settlement. Their mother is a Cherokee of the Wolf Clan, so we must accept them as members of our tribe. This man is Priber. He's not actually a friend of mine, but he asked to come with us to Nequassee to talk with the leaders of our village."

115

"Does he carry a weapon?" the leader asked as he gestured with his hand to have one of his companions search Priber.

"Not that I know of. He has done nothing to hurt us. I think you can trust him."

"I can't find anything," announced the Indian who searched Priber.

"All right. We'll escort you to the village," the leader of the group stated.

"Thank you," said Priber.

"You be quiet," snapped the Cherokee leader. "You may speak to the chief when we get to the village and not before that."

Ela was proud of the strong authority her people held over this white man. She whispered to the leader, "This white man is very strange."

"I don't need any comments from you either, little girl," he responded.

Ela felt as if she had been slapped in the face. She was glad Anna and Johnny had not heard the words. She mumbled to herself, "At least Priber listens to what I have to say."

Ela wondered what the men were doing in that part of the Cherokee countryside. Maybe they had recently gone through her village. They might know if her parents had returned from the hunt safely. In her sweetest voice she said, "Excuse me, I would like to ask you a question." The men did not respond, so she continued, "Do you know if the hunters have returned to my village?"

"They returned a few days ago. We stopped by your village yesterday and helped them to celebrate the success of their hunt, but we had to leave the village early to continue with our own hunting. We were on the trail of a buck when we heard your loud singing. Didn't anyone ever teach you to travel quietly in the forest?"

Ela was embarrassed. She quickly and quietly said to the man, "These people have been very difficult to manage, but I've been doing the best I can."

For the remainder of the afternoon, as the group journeyed to Nequassee, Ela's thoughts centered on home and how wonderful it would be to see her family again. She thought of her friends and how much attention she would receive for her miraculous return.

Finally, Ela started to recognize familiar landmarks along the path — an ancient oak tree as big around as two bears, a rock formation that Ela had always thought resembled a face, and a clearing along the river where she often played as a child. Soon they started passing villagers, whom Ela recognized. Ela called out greetings to each one, and they responded with gasps and exclamations, but the men leading her would not allow Ela to stop and talk.

When her village was within sight, Ela screamed with joy and ran out ahead of the rest, not caring if she was punished for doing so. She knew her parents could protect her now.

The pointed posts that stood closely together, forming a protective fence around the village, were the last barrier between Ela and her house. She pushed through a group of children standing near the gate and ran directly to her home. There it still stood, a tan, mud-covered, boxlike cabin. She remembered how her father and his friends had put up the wooden corner posts and the cross-beams for the framework of the house. Then Mother had woven mats to use as the base for walls. Ela had mixed the mud and grass to apply as plaster over the mats, forming a firm, thick wall when it dried. Before she entered her home, she hesitated. What if her mother and father had not returned from the hunt with the others? What if Grandmother had died from sorrow when she realized Ela was gone? Then her fears melted away as she heard a beautiful voice singing a sad, mournful song.

"Mother!" cried Ela as she entered the cabin. But the interior of the room was so much darker than outside, Ela was unable to see well. There was a small fire in the center of the rectangular room. A movement from the shadows rushed towards her.

"Is it you, Ela? Is it really you?" Ela's mother cried.

"Yes, Mother. I'm home." As they embraced, the love flowing through her mother's arms was almost more than Ela's heart could bear. Tears filled her eyes and trickled down her cheeks onto her mother's shoulder. She had forgotten that her mother could show so much love. It had been a long time since she had felt it. Grandmother had always been the one Ela had depended on in the past. Grandmother. Where was she? Ela looked around the room. Her eyes were becoming accustomed to the darkness. There, in a dark corner, sat Grandmother on a bench. She had a smile on her face.

"So, you remembered me, did you?"

"Oh, yes!" Ela cried as she ran to the old woman and wrapped her arms around her shoulders. "Are you all right? Do you feel well?"

"These old bones ache in their longing for the warm summer days, but my heart is content now that I see you."

Mother came over to Ela and said, "Father isn't here right now, but he will be back later today. When he found out you were gone, he didn't speak for days. He'll be so happy that you have returned to us. Nunda was here last week with a young Catawba brave. When she told us about how cruel the men were who had you, we felt certain we would never see you again."

"Nonsense," retorted Grandmother. "I told you all along that she would return."

"How did you know?" Ela asked.

"I have my ways," replied Grandmother as she crossed her arms over her chest. "A woman my age is very close to the spirit world. You will understand when you are older."

"How did you escape?" asked Mother.

"The horse my guard and I were riding fell down a ravine. The fall killed the Catawba. His friend got away."

"Were you hurt?" asked Mother.

"No, not much, but I was sick for several days. That's how I met Anna and Johnny. They took care of me."

"Who are Anna and Johnny?" Mother asked.

In her haste to see her family, Ela had forgotten all about her new friends and Priber. "They are here in the village. Let me find them and bring them to you."

Ela ran outside and followed the sounds of a large group of villagers gathered at the town gate. When Anna saw Ela she cried, "Ela, come help us." The villagers were crowded in so close to the strangers that Ela was worried Zephyr might get hurt in the crunch.

"Step back. All of you step back. Give my friends some room."

Surprisingly, everyone listened and followed Ela's orders. Tewa shouted from the crowd, "Look, it's Ela."

Now the crowd's attention turned to Ela. As the people pressed in around her, Ela could see that the Cherokee men who had brought her into the village were guiding Anna, Johnny, Zephyr, and Priber toward the cabin of the chief.

"What happened, Ela? How did you get home?" several of her friends cried out.

"I want to tell you, but this isn't the right time. I must make arrangements for the care of my friends first. I'll talk to you later."

"Go back to your work," a village elder named Yunsu called to the group. "We'll learn soon enough about Ela and the strangers." The crowd broke up, and several people groaned with disappointment.

Ela rushed over to the chief's cabin. "Here she is," said one of the braves. "Come here, Ela, and explain who these strangers are." Ela told the men about the role Johnny, Anna, and Priber had played in her return home. She noticed that the chief was not present to hear her story. Where was he? Yunsu, who was acting as the leader, stopped her story when he thought he had heard enough. He ordered that Johnny, Anna, and Zephyr be taken to stay with a widow in the village who had enough room in her cabin. Ela called after them, "Don't worry. I'll see that you get home soon."

"As for you," said Yunsu, looking at Priber, "you will be put in my hot-house from which you cannot easily escape. We will decide what to do with you when the chief returns." He indicated which brave was to guard Priber and take him away.

"Ela," Priber begged, "tell them why I am here. You must. Your tribe may not survive if I am not allowed to live here and help you."

"Silence!" shouted the guard. "You have come uninvited into our village." He led Priber away.

Ela hadn't expected this. Generally, strangers were welcomed into the village. She had hoped the village leaders would listen to what Priber had to say. If they thought he was wrong about the fate of the Cherokee, then they could put him to death. But what if Priber was right? She had to make them give Priber a chance to speak whether she liked the man or not. She started to speak to Yunsu, but he turned away from her.

"This is not the business of little girls," said one of the braves. "Go home." Slowly Ela returned to her cabin. She realized that here, in her village, she was no longer in charge of the situation.

"Where are your friends?" asked Grandmother. "I heard some excitement outside."

"Anna, Johnny, and the baby are with Tuksi's mother, but Yunsu has made Priber a prisoner. The braves won't listen to Priber or me. They need to know that Priber has a plan that would protect our tribal lands from the white men."

Just then, Ela's father strode into the house. "I heard you were back and it's true!" he exclaimed. "Oh, my little Ela," he cried as he lifted her into the air and firmly hugged her. He sat her down next to him. "What is this you were just saying about saving our tribal land?"

Ela told her father the little she knew about Priber and his plan. Then she asked, "Do you think he is a good man or a bad man?"

"It's hard to say," he responded. "You say he has no weapons with him?"

"That's right. He says he only brought books and paper. He promised he would help our people learn to read and write. Maybe he could just stay here long enough to do that. Then we can send him away. Do you think you could convince the village leaders to let him stay?"

"I'll try later, but now it's time to eat," said Father.

"Tomorrow, Ela can introduce us to her new friends," said Mother. "We will have to make arrangements for Anna, Zephyr, and Johnny to get back to their settlement. I'll ask my brother to take them."

The next morning, Ela awakened to the scent of her own home about her. The fragrances from the herbs hanging from the ceiling, the wisps of smoke from burning walnut logs, and the musty buffalo hide covering her, all blended to reassure Ela that she was safe at last.

Grandmother was already awake and sitting on a stool next to the cooking fire, feeding small sticks into it to produce enough heat to keep warm. She moved automatically while peacefully thinking about days gone by.

"Good morning, Grandmother," Ela whispered. The old woman did not hear her, so Ela climbed out of bed and moved over to sit near her grandmother.

"My little Ela is here. Life is finally back to normal," said Grandmother.

Ela kissed the old woman on the top of her head. Just then, Mother and Father began to stir in their bed. Within moments, they were up and getting dressed. As Grandmother had said, life was getting back to normal. Each family member became busy with their usual morning activities. Ela was expected to do the same.

As Ela walked out of her cabin to take her bath in the river, she noticed how the morning sunlight brought out the faint red and green color of the leaf buds on the tips of the trees overhead. There were many other villagers up and about. In the center of the circle of cabins was a clearing with a small circular patch of sand. The circle designated the sacred area where tribal dances and rituals took place. Today, it was empty but it had been used during the hunting celebration held two nights ago. The large council house near the circle was also deserted. At the community storage building, villagers were entering and then leaving with containers filled with corn meal for their morning meals.

Ela strolled down to the river hoping that her old friends would stop what they were doing and notice her. She knew they must be eager to hear about her adventures. They would want her to introduce them to Anna, Johnny, and Zephyr.

Ela's feet seemed to recall the sensation of every root, rock, and hole in the path to the river. She closed her eyes to see how far she could walk without stepping off the path. Ela was doing well until a woman brushed by her and gruffly said, "Watch where you're going, little girl."

Ela wondered how anyone could be so rude. Hadn't she suffered terribly over the past several days? Everyone should be attempting to be kind to her. When Ela arrived at the river, she saw Tewa and ran over to her. "Hello! Did you miss me?"

"Hi, Ela. Sure I missed you. I hope I never get kidnapped. I just started liking Inali. He's so handsome. If I was kidnapped, I would miss him terribly." Tewa spoke with increasing speed and excitement. "Guess what? He kissed me yesterday."

To be polite, Ela smiled with fake enthusiasm, but she was disappointed. Did Tewa only care about herself? Ela decided she wouldn't tell Tewa anything about her adventure unless the selfish girl begged. A few people near the girls waved at Ela, but all went on with their own activities without speaking to her. Ela regretted that she hadn't talked more to her friends the day before while excitement was still in the air.

After bathing, Ela returned to her cabin with lower spirits than she had when the day had started. Mother told Ela at the cabin, "Bring Anna, the baby, and her brother here to have breakfast with us. While you do that, I'll fetch Inadu so he and I can plan their trip home. I'll accompany them part of the way." Ela did as she was told.

When Ela arrived at the widow's cabin, Anna was standing in the doorway. When she saw Ela, she ran to her singing, "We're going home! We're going home!"

"Ela, tell Anna that I'm staying here," Johnny demanded.

"No. You must return with Anna and take care of her. In our tribe, it is the responsibility of a woman's brother to see to it that she and her children are well cared for. You can ask any of the braves here in our village if what I say is not true."

After several moments of silence and pouting, Johnny finally said, "If I have to go home, could I at least bring the blowgun with me?"

"Of course you may," said Ela. She realized that she was going to miss Anna and Johnny. They had saved her life. "Is there anything I can give you to show you my gratitude?" Ela asked Anna.

"You don't need to give me anything. When you saved Johnny, you gave me more than I could ever want again. Maybe you could come and visit us some day. Soon we will be able to write letters to one another, so I hope you learn English quickly."

"I'd like that," Ela admitted.

At breakfast, Anna talked on and on about the way Ela had made weapons and caught food during their journey. She told Ela's parents and grandmother about how brave Ela had been when she rescued Johnny.

"We are very pleased with Ela," Mother said when Anna had completed her story. "It often takes a difficult situation to show us the strength we have within ourselves."

"I feel much older now than I did before my capture," Ela said, "but I don't look any different, and people don't seem to be treating me in a different way."

In her crackly voice, Grandmother said, "Ela, it doesn't matter whether the others notice the change in you, as long as you are aware of it and use your new knowledge."

"We need to take these young people home soon," Inadu said. "There was a white trader in the village yesterday. He said he was on his way to Kanuga. If we hurry, we might catch him and ask for his help. I would take the children all the way home myself, but if a white settler should see me with the children, he might shoot me before giving me a chance to explain my mission."

"Then we must leave quickly. Are you ready?" Father asked.

"Yes."

"Good," said Mother. "Ela, say farewell to your friends."

Ela felt a hollow spot grow in her stomach, though she had just eaten. She didn't want to see her friends leave. When Johnny and Anna were gone, there would be no one left who understood all that she had been through. She hugged Anna and Johnny. Then she asked, "May I hold Zephyr for just a moment?"

"Yes," Anna responded, handing her baby to Ela. Ela cradled the infant lovingly. Why hadn't she held the baby more often while she had the chance? All too quickly Inadu and Father took her friends away. Tears started to roll down Ela's face.

Mother turned to her daughter and said, "It will be planting time soon. Your help is needed to pick rocks out of the cornfield this morning. It will be good for you to keep busy so you won't miss your friends so much. I'll bring some food out to you later. Off you go!"

Back to work already? Ela slowly walked to the field that lay outside the village walls, close to the river. Other children were headed in the same direction, but none came to walk with Ela. Suddenly, she felt like a stranger in her own village. She kept her head down as she picked rock after rock from the soil and threw each into one of the piles that were forming at the edge of the field. She had done this job yearly for as long as she could re-member. How could there still be any rocks left in the field? Was it possible that the soil was so fertile that it could grow rocks? At first, the rocks scratched her hands, but soon her skin was covered with a protective layer of mud.

"Good morning, Ela," said a familiar voice. It was Priber. He selected a spot near Ela and started to help her clear the field.

"What are you doing out here?" Ela asked in surprise.

"My guard told me I would be allowed to leave the hot-house as long as I didn't try to run away. He told me that your father would take the blame if I tried to escape. Did you have something to do with that?" Ela shrugged her shoulders and didn't answer. Priber continued, "I'm sure everyone will learn to accept me when they see that I am trying to help the villagers."

"We'll see," said Ela. Then she asked, "Don't you feel strange being the only adult out here," said Ela.

"Not at all," he responded. "I like to be with children. I have five of my own."

"Where are they?"

"They live with my wife in Germany."

"Don't they need you to be with them?" Ela asked.

"I don't think so. My wife is an artist. She earns enough money to care for the children. Besides, she has lots of relatives to give her money if she needs any."

"Don't you miss your family?"

"Of course I do, but my work has to come first."

"Do you plan to return to Germany some day?"

"No," said Priber. "I have dedicated my life to my dream of creating the Kingdom of Paradise. My wife supports me in this goal. I will bring my family to the kingdom when it is complete."

"You said earlier that you would teach me to speak English. Did you mean it?" Ela asked.

"Certainly. I want to teach all the Cherokee. Now that I think of it, though, it may be smarter to just teach one representative from each village. Then each could be like a missionary and teach the people of his or her own village. That would give me time to work on some other projects I have in mind. You could be the teacher for Nequassee."

This pleased Ela. She agreed to let Priber start teaching her immediately. For the rest of the morning, as they picked rocks out of the soil, Ela and Priber worked on her English lessons. At first, the other children in the field stayed away from them. Most of them seemed to be scared of the white stranger. Eventually, though, some of the older children gradually moved closer. Ela could tell they were trying to hear what she and Priber were talking about, and she hoped they were impressed to hear her speaking foreign words.

Tewa was one of them. "Ela," she asked, "what are you two doing?"

"We're working in the cornfield just like you should be," Ela responded with annoyance.

Tewa quickly bent down to work as she asked questions. "I mean, what are you and that man talking about? I can' t understand him."

"I'm learning to speak English," Ela responded proudly. "This is Priber. Soon he will teach me how to write, too."

"Could he teach me, too?" Tewa asked.

Priber worked quietly while Ela talked to her friend. He looked up a few times to give the other children, who were peering at him, a warm smile, which caused them to look quickly away.

"I'll ask him if he has time to teach you," Ela said to Tewa. But as soon as the words left her mouth, she was sorry, realizing that if the others learned English at the same time, she would no longer be special. Then she felt guilty for feeling this way. A Cherokee wasn't supposed to single herself out from the tribe members. Self-pride was not an acceptable emotion.

Priber spoke out to the children, "It will be too difficult to teach all of you English while we work in the field. I think it would be best if I taught Ela first. Then, she will be your teacher."

Ela couldn't help smiling. The challenge of teaching the others would be exciting. She became more determined to pay close attention to her lessons with Priber so that later she would be a good teacher. Ela would save her pride for her whole village.

By noon, almost half of the field had been cleared and Ela had learned to say, MY NAME IS ELA. THIS IS CHEROKEE LAND. THE CHEROKEE ARE A NOBLE PEOPLE, as well as many phrases that would be useful to her when bargaining with white traders. Priber had explained to Ela how the traders had been cheating the Cherokee over the years, so Ela decided to become a wise businesswoman.

"Time to eat," said Mother as she walked onto the field to catch Ela's attention. She handed Ela a basket filled with food. Mother looked at Priber and back to Ela. "Would you introduce me to your friend?" she asked.

Priber stood up straight and made a little bow at the waist. "Madame, I am Christian Priber. I would like to thank you for the help your family has given me. I expect to make you glad that you did so."

"I'm sure you will," she responded politely.

"Mother," said Ela, "listen to what I can say." Ela repeated some of her English phrases.

"Very good!" Mother exclaimed. "It looks like you two have accomplished a great deal this morning. When you return to the cabin this afternoon, you can tell me more about what you have learned. I'm looking forward to having more time to talk with you, Priber. There's food enough for both you and Ela in the basket. I need to hurry back to bake bean bread for supper." Mother rushed off.

Other mothers came out to the field to feed their children, too, but none tried to speak to Priber. When he and the children were alone again, they all sat on a dry grassy area and ate their meals.

"Tell us about your journey here from Germany," Ela said to Priber.

"I can tell you it was quite an ordeal. I crossed the ocean on a large ship that rocked and rocked until I thought I was going to die of seasickness."

"What is seasickness?" Tewa asked.

Priber answered, "Have you ever twirled around and around until you got very dizzy, and then you felt like you were going to vomit?" Tewa nodded. "That's what it feels like to be seasick," said Priber. Then he continued, "My ship was the size of all your canoes lined up in a row and as wide as three of your cabins." The eyes of the children opened wide in amazement. "Have any of you children seen the ocean?" They all shook their heads. "Well, the ocean is like a giant river that is bigger than all of the Cherokee Nation." There were sounds of awe from the listeners. "It took the ship more than two weeks to cross the ocean."

Priber found a stick and drew a crude map of Europe and America. When he showed the children how small an area the Cherokee Nation held in the world, many of the children stood up with anger and refused to believe anything else the man had to say. But Ela believed him. She had already traveled farther from the village than any of the other children. As she looked at the map, she couldn't help but realize how vulnerable her people were to invaders.

"It's hopeless," Ela cried. "We're doomed. I don't know why you came here. The Cherokee people will never be able to protect their land from so many enemies."

The children who had remained to listen all looked worried. "Are we going to be killed?" a young boy asked his older brother. The older boy shrugged his shoulders and looked to Ela for reassurance.

Priber answered for Ela. "I've told Ela that I'm here to bring your people the knowledge you need to help you stand strong against the white settlers. You can do it, I am sure."

The little boy asked his brother, "Do you understand him?"

"I'm not sure. I think I do, though."

"Let me explain myself this way," Priber continued. "In your tribe, each member is important to village life. Each person, like you," he said, pointing to the little boy, "has work to do to help your people survive. That's why you're working here today. You'll learn more skills from your elders as you grow older. The more you learn, the more the other villagers will treat you with respect. If you refuse to learn how to participate in tribal business as an adult, the elders will make all your decisions for you. You will have no say in your future."

Ela was starting to understand. She told the children, "He's trying to say that if we decide to learn how to do business with the rest of the world in a way that is respected by them, the white men would not try to take advantage of us and steal our land. We will be able to make our own decisions about what will happen to our land."

"That's right," said Priber. The children seemed relieved that the discussion was over. It was time to go back to work in the field.

Ela and Priber worked side by side for a long time before either of them spoke. Ela needed quiet time to think. In some ways, she wished her life had remained as it was before her kidnapping. She had always taken the flow of village life for granted. Back then it was as though she was a leaf that was being carried by a gentle current in the river. Now, Ela felt caught in a whirlpool of emotions, and she was struggling to reach a point of safety that did not exist.

"Do you really think that you can help us?" Ela finally asked Priber.

"Yes, I do. And I think that you will play an important role in saving your nation. You have already demonstrated great courage and intelligence. If you are willing to work hard and are willing to stand up for the rights of your people, you will be a great help."

Ela was surprised at how confident Priber was. Just this morning, Mother had expressed the same confidence in Ela. It would be difficult to live up to their expectations, but it was better than sitting helplessly by as her nation faced danger.

"I'm ready to learn more English," Ela informed Priber. He taught her for the rest of the afternoon while they finished their work in the field. When the work was done, several young boys invited Priber to watch them play stickball. Girls were not invited to play, so Priber stood with Ela and her friends to watch. Each boy held a stick that was slightly shorter than himself. At one end of the stick was a hand-sized net. With this stick and net, the boys were able to throw and catch a small ball. The young boys practiced their skills seriously, knowing that when they became men, they would play on the village team and enter competitions with other Cherokee villages or even those of other tribes. In the games, the two teams would stand at opposite ends of a field, facing each other and try to pass the ball with their sticks from one of their team members to another, running toward a goal in the other team's territory. In the meantime, the opponents would try to steal the ball away by intercepting it or knocking the ball-carrier down with their stick. Bones were often broken.

One of the boys convinced Priber to try his hand at stickball. The children laughed hysterically as the clumsy man missed his targets and dropped the balls thrown to him, but he didn't seem to mind. He laughed louder at himself than the children did.

Priber looked over at Ela and gave her a friendly smile. Tewa jabbed Ela in the ribs and giggled. "I think he likes you," she whispered.

Ela's face turned red. "Don't be silly, Tewa," she retorted. "Of course, he likes me. I'm his friend." Ela knew that Tewa meant something different, but she refused to consider the possibility that Priber could like her in any way other than a friend.

CHAPTER ELEVEN

Late the following afternoon, Ela, Priber, and the village children were clearing a different field. Suddenly, Ela noticed that some of the children near her had stopped working. She looked around to see what had caught their attention. Four braves, led by their chief, were marching from the village gate toward Ela and Priber. Children instinctively stepped away from the area where Ela and Priber stood so that they would not get involved in whatever was causing their elders to look so serious. Ela stayed by Priber's side, though she longed to run and hide. She didn't want to know why the village elders were angry.

"Seize him," the chief ordered. Priber didn't put up a fight, but still the braves treated him roughly, knocking him to the ground and binding his hands and feet.

"I'm your friend," Priber shouted as he lay helplessly on the ground. "I've done nothing wrong. I'm here to help you."

"Gag him," the chief responded, and one of the braves followed his command. "Take him back to the hot-house and leave him there. He will be executed in the morning."

"No!" cried Ela.

"Take this girl home to her family," the chief instructed another brave. The brave pulled Ela by her arm toward the village as the other braves carried Priber like a captured mountain lion.

As they entered the gates, Nunda, who was in tears, rushed to Ela's side. "Priber's friends killed Essabo and one of our Cherokee braves as they were returning with Father from Tellico. They were ambushed. Father only survived because the white men were too scared to stay and fight like real men. Their deaths must be avenged."

Ela was shocked. Nunda must have been referring to the white hunters who had captured Johnny. Priber was in serious trouble now since murder had to be avenged. It might not matter that Priber didn't know the murderers. Ela didn't want to lose Priber. He wasn't a friend like someone her own age could be, but he had always been considerate and helpful to Ela, and he was a good teacher.

Ela knew what would happen to Priber. He would be carried out to the village square in the morning. Splinters of wood would be poked into his skin on the front of his body, making him look like a porcupine. Then a warrior would light the splinters and the whole village would watch as the splinters burned down to Priber's skin, burning a small area of skin at the base of each. Priber would be turned over and the same torture would take place on his other side. Finally, he would be thrown into the bonfire that was ignited for the occasion. That type of torture was not new to Ela. She had attended several in the past. The elders thought it was important for children to become used to seeing their enemies punished. Most of the time it was the women of the tribe who took over the torturing tasks, but for Priber the men would probably be present.

Ela's mother was waiting for her at the cabin door. "Mother, they're going to kill Priber," Ela cried. Mother quickly brought Ela into the cabin and made a hushing sound so that Ela would say no more in front of the neighbors. Once inside, Ela said, "Mother, we've got to do something." Ela began to pace back and forth. She tried to push away her feelings of helplessness and remember the strength she now knew she had. "I must convince the elders to have a tribal meeting before they kill Priber."

"Now, Ela, they might not kill him. Maybe they will just send him away from here."

"Please don't try to make me feel better when I know what will happen. Can we organize some kind of protest?"

Grandmother spoke up from her corner of the room. "Maybe I could make them listen to me."

Of course! Grandmother was the "Beloved Woman" of the village. Only she, of all women, had the power to influence the decisions of the men in the tribal council. "If we get the other women in the tribe to insist on being heard before a decision is made, then a meeting might be called."

"What do you recommend?" Ela's mother asked.

"Tomorrow morning, when Priber is being prepared for torture, I can try to order them to stop. It would be helpful if I had the support of the other women in the tribe. Ela, you and your mother must talk to our women friends to convince them that Priber should live. What do you think would be a good reason to give them that would make them willing to give up their enjoyment of having an execution?"

"We could tell them how important Priber is to the education of their children. We could say that our village will have the most knowledgeable people in the mountains, and we can be of better service to the Cherokee Nation."

"That would be good enough for me," said Mother. "Let's go now, Ela. You talk to the young women and I'll talk to the older ones." Supper was left sitting near the fire as the two hurried to spread the word.

Ela found many of the young women gathered near the hot-house. Nunda stood with them. All were chattering like blue jays about the upcoming execution. Ela wondered what she could say to them. She knew that Nunda was their leader, and she realized from past experience that to get on Nunda's good side, she should flatter her.

"Nunda, I'm so glad I found you and your friends. I have something important to ask you."

"You cannot ask me to convince my father to free Priber," Nunda stated. Her friends nodded in agreement.

"I understand how angry you must be," said Ela, "but I want you to be sure you have considered some important facts. Priber did not know the men who killed Essabo. I believe that if Priber was allowed to teach us to read and write, we would be one of the most honored villages in our tribe. Cherokee would come from near and far to see what we have learned. Then any one of you," said Ela pointing to all the young women, "would probably have her choice of any man in the Cherokee tribe for a husband."

Nunda wasn't responding. Ela could tell she was thinking about herself and not her friends. How could the beautiful maiden, even in her grief, pass up the opportunity to flirt with more men. Finally, with much prodding from friends to speak, Nunda said, "I don't think I can make Father change his mind."

"I'm not asking you to take on that task alone." Then, speaking to all the maidens, Ela said, "My grandmother has agreed to speak up at the execution tomorrow and demand that Priber not be killed. It will be important for all of you to show your support for her. My mother will make sure that your mothers support us, too. When she asks for your votes to decide whether to kill Priber or not, you need to shout out your objection to the execution.

"What harm could it do?" one of the maidens asked her friends.

"No harm at all," said Ela, trying to reassure the young women. "Just remember, when you go back home tonight, don't mention a word of this to anyone. We are more likely to get our way if we don't give the men a chance to think of a way to overrule us."

"But the men will insist on revenge," Tewa pointed out.

"Priber probably has the power to call on white soldiers to capture the murderers and have them punished," Ela said. The maidens talked among themselves and then agreed to help.

The next morning, Ela rushed through her morning tasks so that she could get home in time to prepare for the execution. Other villagers seemed to hurry with an underlying excitement. No one spoke to Ela, but she saw several people whispering to each other and pointing in her direction. She just held her head up proudly and returned to her cabin to eat breakfast.

Ela said to Grandmother, "Are you ready to speak to the villagers?"

"I think so," Grandmother answered, "but are you ready to defend Priber, too?"

"We have the support of the maidens. Is that what you mean?"

"Not exactly. If you had to speak to the elders about your reasons to spare Priber, would you be able to do so?"

Ela felt nervous all of a sudden. "I thought you would take care of everything," Ela said.

"I'm willing to help you as much as I can, Ela, but you must be clear about what benefits Priber can provide to our whole tribe, not just individuals within the tribe. We are all linked to each other and must keep the welfare of the group above the welfare of one or two people."

Ela thought about all the reasons she had for wanting Priber to live. She had thought of the status that she would gain and of the status her town might gain, but would Priber be good for the whole Cherokee Nation? How could she ever be sure?

Just then Ela heard a drumbeat from the town square. She turned to her mother and nervously asked, "Are we doing the right thing?"

"What do you feel deep down in your heart?"

"I think we need Priber to help our people stand up to the white people. Otherwise, we may lose all our land."

"Then I trust that we are doing the right thing," said Mother. She picked up a small buffalo robe and wrapped it around Grandmother's shoulders. "Time to go."

The old woman took the buffalo robe off. "Let me wear the woolen blanket. This buffalo robe weighs me down and I don't want to appear all bent over like a helpless old woman." So Ela put her own red blanket around Grandmother. The three walked to the village square together with a look of determination.

Priber had already been put in position for torture. He lay in a large, long basket set on the ground. His hands and feet were still bound, but his mouth was ungagged. His eyes were wide open with fear, and his lips were moving in rapid prayer. Within moments, every villager had arrived. The chief stood to one side of the square, accompanied by several of the important village leaders. He raised his right hand, held it in the air for a few moments until everyone became very quiet. Then he nodded his head toward the woman who would be the one to begin the torture. Priber closed his eyes in terror. Ela looked at her grandmother with expectation.

In the anticipatory hush, Grandmother shouted out, "Stop!" All eyes turned toward the old woman. Even Priber opened his eyes to see.

"What is the problem?" the chief called to her.

"It is customary to ask the Beloved Woman what she wants done with a captive. Has it been so long since the last execution that you do not remember this?"

The men in the village looked at one another in confusion. Then the chief said, "What do you want us to do, Beloved Woman?"

"I say that Priber should be released and allowed to live among us."

"Will you deprive the women in the tribe of the honor of killing this man?" the chief asked Grandmother.

Grandmother called out in her loudest voice, which was not very loud, "Tell the chief how you feel, my sisters?" She immediately started coughing and held her throat as though the strain on her voice was too much.

Cries came from all the women and maidens of the village to let Priber live. Ela turned to her grandmother and embraced her.

The chief looked concerned. "We must all agree on what to do with the white man. It will not do to have all women feel one way about the decision and the men feel another way. Walk over here, Beloved Woman, and tell us why we men should agree with you."

Grandmother tried to speak but was unable to. She whispered to Ela, "You tell him, my voice is gone. Tell him I have selected you to speak for me."

Ela sucked in a quick breath. "Me?" Grandmother nodded.

"What does she say, young one?" asked the chief. Ela told him.

"This is highly unusual," said the chief. He spoke quietly to the man beside him for a moment, then said, "Come forward, Ela of the Bird Clan. You, who have brought this white man into our village, tell us why he should be allowed to live."

Mother gave Ela a little push. Ela walked slowly to the center of the square. Hesitantly, she said, "Priber could tell you better than I could."

"Priber has no right to speak to us yet," said the chief. "Have you nothing to say? If you haven't, then we must choose a way to dispose of him that is agreeable to everyone."

"Oh, no. I want to speak," said Ela. The chief crossed his arms in front of his chest and waited. All the villagers looked at Ela. Ela looked at Grandmother who gave her a nod of confidence. Then Ela looked at Priber. He gave Ela a pleading stare, for his life was in her hands.

Ela started, "I believe Priber should be allowed to live among us in the Cherokee Nation. I have been told that our nation will dwindle in size as the white settlers hunger for more land. Is this true?" Ela asked the chief.

"It is possible, but how can you be sure Priber will not help them take more land?"

"I don't think Priber can do anything that we don't want him to do. He is one man. We are many Cherokee. Priber has many plans of his own to help our tribe and other Indian tribes, but we have the power to decide how much we will allow him to do. He is not asking that we sign a treaty."

"Why should we let him carry out any of his plans? We have done well without him," said the chief.

"I think we could do better with the white men if we understood their language and their writing. Priber is willing to teach our whole nation to speak, read, and write English. He has already taught me many words." Then Ela spoke several sentences in English.

The chief turned again to his advisors. They spoke several minutes while the villagers waited, straining their ears to hear what the men were saying. Finally, the chief turned to the villagers. "It seems that Priber intends to make changes that will affect our whole nation. It is best that we take him to Great Tellico and present him to a meeting of tribal leaders that is to be held there in a few days. I will appoint two of our braves and Ela to accompany Priber to Great Tellico starting tomorrow morning. Priber will be allowed to discuss his plans to the tribal leaders, and Ela will demonstrate what she has learned. We will leave it up to the tribal leaders to decide if he should stay among us as a teacher or be sent back to his people. Does anyone disagree with this?"

The villagers stood silently.

"Then release the prisoner," the chief ordered.

Tewa and the other maidens ran up to Ela and congratulated her. Nunda said, "When you return from Great Tellico, would you teach me how to speak English?"

"Me too. Me too," the other maidens chimed in.

"I'd be happy to teach you all I know, but I still have a lot to learn before I can be much help." Then Ela remembered Priber. She went to help him get out of the basket. His legs were shaking, but he had a smile on his face.

"Thank you, Ela. I promise that you will never be sorry that you helped me."

Mother and Grandmother joined them. Mother said to Priber, "We have made arrangements for you to stay at my friend's house tonight so that you won't have to spend anymore time in that hot-house."

"You are very kind," Priber responded. "As for the rest of today, is there more work to do in the fields?" Ela was amazed that a man so close to death should be ready to get back to work again. "Don't you want to get your belongings ready for our trip tomorrow?" Ela asked.

"I am ready to travel, and I am ready to work," he said.

"You and Ela should go ahead back to work," said Mother. The other children are already on their way to the fields. Ela, I will prepare a traveling pack for you."

So Ela and Priber returned to the fields, and for the rest of the day the children of the tribe worked as closely to them as possible so they could hear more stories from Priber and listen to Ela's English lessons. Little Sister hopped about on the edges of the field, sensing the excitement of the workers. She came close enough for some of the small children to throw her little pieces of their mid-day meal.

CHAPTER TWELVE

When Ela opened her eyes the next morning, she was surprised to see Grandmother sitting next to her. No one else was awake.

"Is anything wrong, Grandmother?"

"No."

"Why are you sitting here?"

"I'm thinking about how quickly you are growing."

"I'll still be your granddaughter forever and ever," Ela swore. She raised herself and gently kissed her grandmother's cheek.

"Nothing is forever, my little Ela. I will soon pass on to the spirit world."

"Don't say that, Grandmother," Ela pleaded.

"It's all right," Grandmother assured her. "I have lived a long life. I'm not afraid of death. I just worry about how you and your children will be able to manage the changes that time will bring to our nation."

"What do you mean?"

"Our people have had to give up most of our best hunting grounds in the low lands just to keep peace with the white man. Still he wants more. Sometimes, I feel he is trying to push us off of this earth."

"We can stop them if we listen to Priber."

"That might be true, but the white settlers come over our land like a great wind that can't be stopped. Like the wind, the white men who come here have no roots, and they seem destined to wander aimlessly forever, always looking for something better over the next mountain. But we Cherokee are part of this land. Our roots are our history, our customs, our stories, and our loyalty to one another. We belong to this land more than the land belongs to us." Then Grandmother gave Ela a sly smile. "Won't the white men be furious when they find they can never take all that is ours? How can anyone steal our history and traditions?"

"Grandmother, I don't want them to take anything that is ours, but it may not be so bad to continue trading our goods for theirs. Is it bad that I want some of the things the white people have?"

"What do you want?"

"I want a new blanket for you. I want metal tools to make work in the fields easier. I want to have clothes made from woven fabric so my clothes will be warmer and not so heavy."

"My dear, the things you want cannot hurt anyone. Life is difficult for us. There is nothing wrong with trying to make your family's life a bit easier. However, you need to be aware of the precious possessions you already have. When we are children, we pay little attention to the gifts the Great Spirit has given us because we assume they will always be with us. In some ways, it is good that Priber has talked to you about why he wants to live with us. He's bringing to light the good things about our nation that have been difficult to describe before."

"He told me that he wants to have a nation where all people help each other, where no one goes hungry, where everyone works for the good of the community," said Ela.

"We already live that way, Ela. That's why you work as hard as you do in the field. That's why we have a community food storage building. No one goes hungry in our nation unless all the Cherokee go hungry."

"He said that he wants a nation where people are not put into a prison or killed for small mistakes they had made in their lives."

"Among our own people, the only ones who are executed are those who have killed a fellow Cherokee. Even then, the only reason for that is so there will never be battles between clans to seek revenge for wrongs done to each other. Any other crime that a person commits is handled with a brief public humiliation. Then, each year, every misdeed is forgotten with the Green Corn ceremony and the lighting of the new Sacred Fire."

"Then, Priber has chosen our nation for his plans because he won't have to work so hard to make his paradise a reality?"

"It looks that way," said Grandmother. "He is a smart man. Don't hesitate to get the information from him that you want, for we have given him a fair exchange already. Our way of life has great value." Then Grandmother stood up and walked slowly out of the cabin. Ela thought about what the old woman had said. Tradition had always been important to the elders of the tribe, and children were expected to honor these traditions. Most older adults resented any changes that other tribal members might want to make in their society, but Grandmother seemed to be aware that changes were going to happen whether she wanted them to or not. Ela understood her own new responsibility, to help direct the changes that would be needed to help her tribe.

When Mother and Father awakened, Mother gave Ela a surprise. She laid a new deerskin skirt on Ela's bed.

"Go ahead, Ela," said Father. "Try it on."

Quickly, Ela wrapped the skirt around her slim waist.

"You look beautiful," said Father. "Soon you will be as lovely as your mother." Mother gave Father a hug. Father continued, "I'll go outside and see if the chief is ready to leave. You need to eat a hearty meal and put on your leggings and moccasins."

"My moccasins are ruined, but don't worry. I'll go barefoot. The weather is getting nice and warm."

Grandmother overheard Ela as she entered the cabin. "Your feet are the same size as mine. You must wear my old moccasins. After all, I have the nice new pair you made for me." Grandmother handed Ela a finely stitched pair that were much nicer than the pair Ela had given her. When she tried to tell Grandmother so, the old woman insisted that Ela take the good pair.

Ela slipped the moccasins on. Then she slowly wrapped her deerskin leggings around the calves of her legs, tying them in place around her ankles and knees with garters of braided fibers. Mother combed Ela's waist-long black hair as Ela ate her bowl of mush. Then Mother reached for a leather pouch that was hanging on the wall. Out of it she pulled a long, red, silky ribbon.

"Where did you get that?" Ela asked, her eyes wide with surprise.

"I was saving this for your wedding day. But, it seems best to give it to you now. It will look so lovely with what you are wearing." She tied it into Ela's hair. The ribbon looked bright as flame against the ebony background of her hair.

"I love you," Ela said to her mother. "I'm sorry that I have to leave you again already, but I'm excited at the same time."

"I know what you mean," Mother said as she looked off into the distance with dreamy eyes. "There are many adventures out there in the world to experience. I'm glad you have the chance to see new places and learn new skills. Before long, you will have your own children and will be unable to leave them to go adventuring."

Ela had never thought of the possibility that it was motherhood that had kept her mother from being a more interesting person. Suddenly, Ela felt guilty.

"Do you wish you had explored the world before you had me?" Ela asked.

"I'm glad everything happened just the way it did," said Mother with a loving smile. "I'm not too old to start living some of my dreams. You are almost full grown. When you come back from Great Tellico, you will teach me English. Then we can visit some of the big cities I have heard of. I want to see the big sailing ships that carry people over the ocean."

"I'll take you to see them, Mother. I promise."

Soon it was time to leave. Father, Mother, and Grandmother stood a slight distance away from where the chief, Priber, the braves, and Ela were organizing themselves. One horse was to be used for the journey. The traveling packs were tied to him. Priber had his big traveling chest to carry, but the braves had already assured him that they would help as needed.

"Let's go," the chief ordered.

Ela quickly looked back at her family and at the few friends that had come out to see the travelers leave. "I'll be back soon!" she called to them.

"We'll be here waiting for you," Father responded. Mother and Grandmother waved. Grandmother looked so old and feeble that Ela wondered if she would ever see her again. Ela turned to face future and that of the Cherokee Nation — without fear.

HISTORICAL EPILOGUE

Ela was a fictitious character in this story, though she symbolizes the countless Native Americans who showed great courage in trying to keep the European settlers from destroying their nation. Christian Priber was a real character in American history. When Priber reached Great Tellico, he was accepted by Moytoy, the primary chief of the Cherokee. Priber convinced the Cherokee leaders to avoid taking sides with either the French or the British in the white man's battle to rule North America. In that way the Cherokee could trade with both nations and avoid any retaliation.

Priber encouraged the Cherokee to take the ownership of their lands seriously. Previously, the Cherokee felt that no man could own the earth, just as it was impossible to claim the air in the sky as one's own. Priber pressed the Indians to band together in strength to present themselves as a separate nation from but equal to the white man's colonies.

Priber kept detailed notebooks of his philosophies and activities. More importantly, it is claimed that he wrote a dictionary of the Cherokee language which he showed to a few white travelers who came through Great Tellico.

The British and the French both thought of Priber as a menace. Several times soldiers were sent into the Cherokee Nation to seize Priber, but the Cherokee guarded him well. Finally, in 1743, while on a journey to what is now Alabama, Priber was captured by a group of Creek Indians and frontiersmen hired by the British for that purpose. He was put in prison, where he died one year later. There is no information on how he died. His notebooks and dictionary were lost. Many historians feel that Christian Priber was one of the first white men to try to do something to help the Cherokee.

After Priber's death, the following years brought many injustices to the Cherokee. Many treaties were made between the Native Americans and the colonists in which the Cherokee agreed to give the white men parts of their territory under the condition that the new boundaries would be honored. Each and every time the white men broke those treaties until finally, in 1838, the entire Cherokee tribe was ordered to leave their land and move to what is now Oklahoma. Twelve thousand men, women, and children walked almost one thousand miles to their new home, a six-month journey, during which over 400 Cherokee died. Some historians claim that the overall number of Cherokee who died in events related to their removal from their homeland was close to 4,000. Their tragic journey is now called the "Trail of Tears."

About 1,400 Cherokee remained in the East. There were several hundred Cherokee who had legally bought land from white landholders outside of the Cherokee boundary. This group was called the Qualla band of Cherokee. They had not been ordered to leave North Carolina. Cherokee who had helped the U.S. government round up their brethren for removal were allowed to stay with the Qualla band. Those Cherokee who had hidden in mountain caves to avoid removal were also allowed to eventually settle with the Qualla band. Together the Eastern band of the Cherokee Nation appointed William Holland Thomas — a white man adopted in his youth by a Cherokee chief — to buy more land for the

Eastern Cherokee, since Cherokee were no longer allowed to buy land for themselves. Eventually, they acquired 57,000 acres in the western corner of North Carolina. Their land, named the Qualla Boundary, is often referred to as the Cherokee Reservation. Today, however, the majority of the almost 100,000 members of the Cherokee Nation live on a vast reservation in northeastern Oklahoma.

FOR YOUR INFORMATION

This book includes a map of the boundary of Cherokee Nation lands in the year 1735. The Cherokee lands included most of what is now Tennessee, Kentucky, and parts of West Virginia, North Carolina, South Carolina, Georgia, and Alabama. Ela's village is Nequassee, or what is now known as Franklin, North Carolina. Her journey took her to the northwestern corner of South Carolina near a little town that was then known as Sugar Town. There is no town in that location now. Ela was planning to travel to Great Tellico at the end of this story. Tellico was located in what is now known as eastern Tennessee. Tellico was a central meeting place for Cherokee village leaders where they made many major decisions, including the signing of treaties with European colonists.

Other tribes are mentioned in this story. They include the Creek, the Catawba, and the Tuscarora. Catawba territory lay to the east of Cherokee land in the Piedmont area of central North Carolina. The Catawba tribe was smaller than the Cherokee and Creek tribes. They often battled with the Cherokee to the west and Tuscarora to the east. When the colonists first started seizing native lands, the Catawba joined their former enemies, the Cherokee and Tuscarora, to fight the white people. But soon the

Catawba were forced to become allies of the colonists to avoid being annihilated, so they became enemies of the Cherokee again. Today, the Catawba have a tiny reservation in northern South Carolina and disputes over their lands occur even today.

The Tuscarora inhabited eastern North Carolina and South Carolina. The Tuscarora War, a war between the Tuscarora and South Carolina white settlers, took place from 1711-1713. The Tuscarora were defeated and most were moved to New York. Those Tuscarora who had remained neutral during the war were allowed to stay in North Carolina. There they continued warfare with their enemies, the Catawba, and occasionally they raided white settlements to get supplies. In 1802, the North Carolina Tuscarora were pressured to join their people on New York and Ontario reservations.

The major territory of the Creeks was what is now the state of Alabama and part of western Georgia. The Creeks were the sworn enemies of the Cherokee through most of their history even before the Europeans came to settle in America. As settlers took over more and more Native American land, the Creeks eventually joined with the Cherokee in the late 1700's to fight the settlers. In 1827, the Creeks gave up all their remaining lands in the Southeast and moved to their reservation in Oklahoma, adjacent to the Oklahoma Cherokee Reservation.